Biscuits and Bodies:
Alphabet Soup Mysteries

Book 2

Erica J Whelton

Publisher: Sunseri Design Publishing
Cover Designer: Mariah Sinclair Book Cover Design
ISBN: 978-1-956069-26-6

Printed in the United States of America

To my beautiful, supportive friend, Stacy.
Thank you for all the years of friendship.
Now on to our "golden" years!

Books in this series:

Appetizers and Alibis (Book 1)
Biscuits and Bodies (Book 2)
Cornbread and Coffins (Book 3)
Dumplings and Disaster (Book 4)

Other books by this author:

<u>Paranormal Cozy Mystery</u>
Premedicated Murder: Medium with a Heart (book 1)
Replicated Murder: Medium with a Heart (book 2)
Organized Murder: Medium with a Heart (book 3)
Inherited Murder: Medium with a Heart (book 4)
Crafted Murder: Medium with a Heart (book 5)
Destined Murder: Medium with a Heart (book 6)

<u>Small-town Women's Fiction</u>
Mandy's Story: Courage – Finding Herself Series (book 1)
Becca's Story: Purpose – Finding Herself Series (book 2)
Caroline's Story: Serenity – Finding Herself Series (book 3)

The Haunting of Anna-Rose (Paranormal Suspense)
Decoding Us (Women's Fiction/Friendship)

Chapter One

I stared into my closet. I hadn't been on a date in years. My stomach fluttered, which was silly. This wasn't a romantic date exactly. It was more of a thank you to Colt, Noah's friend, for his help with finding Earl's killer and helping to find who had been trying to sabotage my business.

But after texting with him the past week as we made plans, I was truly interested in getting to know him. He had a dark and dry sense of humor, like mine. We both liked the same music, and he was into art.

Plus, you never know what could happen after a first date.

I felt my cheeks warm at the thought. I was thankful I had my back turned to my friends. Vee could usually read me like a book, so if I could just avoid her eyes for a moment, she wouldn't know.

I flipped through a few of my shirts, stopping on my newest t-shirt.

"I don't think a Neal Barney shirt is the right outfit for a first date, right?" I turned to ask Vee and Sawyer, my best friends and roommates.

Neal Barney was a local artist who created folk art shirts. We were probably his biggest fans. I had five shirts with his illustrations on them. My favorite was probably my bigfoot one, or maybe the witch with her black cat. Who am I kidding? I loved them all.

"Do you have anything else?" Vee asked, joining me to flip through my clothes.

She grabbed a floral dress, holding it out for me to inspect. I gave it a thumbs down.

"Not even sure why I kept that monstrosity."

It looked like a tent on me. I think I'd bought it for some function my grandmother made me go to with her. I wore it exactly once.

Then, she pulled out a navy blouse, but I wasn't going to an interview, so it felt like too much. We added it to the pile of rejects on the bed in front of me. I really didn't have a lot of appropriate date clothes.

"Ugh, why is this so hard?" I groaned. "I should have gone shopping."

"Oh, wait! What about that red shirt with the silver stripes?" Vee blurted.

She looked around the bed for it while I flipped through the closet, holding it out when I found it.

"Um, this one." I hadn't worn it in a few years. "I'm not sure if it still fits."

"Only one way to find out," Vee said, gesturing for me to take my shirt off.

I groaned, pulling off my t-shirt then slipping into the red one. It felt okay. I turned toward the mirror. It actually fit a little loose. That was a pleasant surprise, and here I'd thought I'd gained weight.

"What do y'all think?" I modeled for them.

"Nice," Vee said.

Sawyer whistled, giving a thumbs up.

"But what do I wear with it, pants or maybe a skirt?" I turned back to the closet.

"With your black jeans and those ankle boots," Sawyer added.

I grabbed the jeans and boots, slipping into them. I turned a few times, showing off for them.

"That's it."

"You look beautiful."

"Thanks. I think this is what I'll wear." I checked myself in my full-length mirror. It was surprisingly flattering. I loved it. "Okay. This works."

My phone chimed. It was Noah asking how I was and if I was ready for my date.

Me: **I think so.**

N: **No backing out, Chef**

I laughed.

"It's Noah," I said to my friends.

"Aw, he's excited for you." Vee laughed.

"He has been a downright pest about this."

I know he wanted to make a love connection for his two friends, but I just didn't see this as a romantic thing. Colt was nice, and we had some fun texting conversations, but I didn't see a relationship here. Friendship maybe.

So why was I putting so much thought into what I was going to wear? Why were there butterflies in my stomach? I put my hand on my stomach, trying to settle it.

"Are you nervous?" Vee giggled.

I wanted to lie, but I knew she'd see right through my hollow words.

"Of course." I chuckled. "I mean, he seems nice. But I'm mostly nervous because I haven't been on any kind of date in years."

"Not since ... what was his name?"

"Chuck." I groaned. That had been a crash and burn moment. He'd put me off dating and I hadn't even considered it until now.

"Chuck." They said in unison.

"He was awful," Vee said.

"He thought he was funny, but it was mostly hurtful jokes at my expense, and he had been rude to Aunt Rita. Nobody is rude to my favorite aunt."

"He was a pig." Vee made a face but then smiled. "Well, I'm happy that you are getting out there again."

"Me too," Sawyer said as he stood. "Well, I'm off for my date. Can't wait to hear about yours."

He leaned over, kissing us both on our cheeks.

"Have fun," we yelled after him.

"Make good choices," Vee added.

"Not on your life," he yelled back.

We laughed as we heard him close the front door.

"So, what're you doing tonight?" I asked.

"Oh, you know, me and Netflix have a hot date. I might invite Lulu, so she doesn't miss you too much." Vee scratched the cat's belly. Lulu was my cat, but she loved us all, especially Sawyer.

"She'll love that."

I finished my make-up and hair, then added a long necklace with a silver geometric design at the end. I checked my image once more. Perfect. I think I'm ready.

"You look beautiful. I hope you have the best time." She walked me downstairs.

"Thanks." I hugged her. "Alright, see ya later."

I jogged down the stairs to my car.

I sent him a text.

Me: **On my way**.

C: **Great! I'm heading that way in 5**

I smiled as I put my car in drive, then headed to A Dash and A Pinch Bistro. This was a new restaurant that had opened not long after mine, and I was eager to try it. I'd heard good things about it.

It was close to where Colt lives so he planned to walk there. My stomach fluttered again when I thought of him.

Now that Parker and June could handle things at my restaurant, and the murder of Earl had been solved, I could take time off for just me. It was a nice change. I felt lighter and like things were finally falling into place.

As I got near the bistro, I started looking for street parking. Most of the parking in and around Dashwood, especially here near the downtown area, was street parking. However, I didn't find any, so I circled the block coming up on the other side. A little surprising for a Sunday night. I assumed, obviously wrongly, that the patrons would have been workers on lunch breaks, so I thought restaurants would mostly be busy during the workweek.

Thankfully, I managed to find a spot about a block away, but still in sight of the restaurant. Once I was parked, I looked over my shoulder.

I think Colt lives back that way. I smiled, as I pulled my phone out to message him.

Me: **Here**.

He didn't reply, so I assumed he was on his way, though I didn't see him on the street. Perhaps he was already inside and didn't hear his phone.

I walked to A Dash and A Pinch Bistro. It was a cute place on the corner of a line of shops. They were lucky to get an end, because it allowed them to do some patio style seating.

I had a corner spot also, but I also had a parking lot, so no space for a patio. It would have been nice to have, but I liked my cozy interior.

"Hi, welcome to A Dash and A Pinch," the host greeted. "Table for one?"

"No, two. I'm meeting someone." I looked around the small space. "It doesn't look as if he's here yet. Though he should be here any second."

I scanned the room once more. We had sent each other pictures. He wasn't the 'hot guy,' but cute with a teddy bear look about him, which I loved. He had red hair, green eyes, and was tall like me.

"Okay, great. I can get you seated. Inside or out?"

After working in a hot kitchen all day, I wanted to sit in the air conditioning, especially when it is so humid out like now.

"Inside, please?"

"Right this way." She grabbed two menus and two bundles of silverware.

As I followed her, it gave me the opportunity to check out the competition. It looked like a sixty top restaurant squashed together. I would have only tried to fit maybe forty tables max in here, instead of the sixty it was now.

There wasn't a lot of space between tables. If people were sitting back-to-back, they would potentially bump into each other, and nobody could walk between tables comfortably. Reducing it by at least twenty would give that space to walk.

I loved how mine was roomy. Nothing worse than feeling like you are eating with strangers. I guess some people don't mind that, but I was not one of those people. I liked a little space and privacy, especially on a first date.

"Here you are. Your server will be right with you."

"Thanks." I settled and then checked my phone. No text yet, so I sent him one.

Me: **Got us a table**

"Hi, I'm your server Ashley. Are you waiting for someone?"

"Yes, he'll be here any minute."

"Do you want to wait for him, or would you like a drink?"

"Um, let me start with an iced tea. Thanks."

"Great. Coming right up."

From here I could see out the window facing down the street. I leaned over to see if I could see him. Nobody on the street. Next, I checked my phone again; the volume was on, but it didn't look like he'd read my messages yet. I thought he said he was going to walk over, which in my mind meant he could read his texts.

Maybe it was in his pocket, and he just didn't hear it, I thought, shifting in the seat. *Boy, I'm nervous.* I smoothed my hair.

Ashley brought my iced tea. "Sweetener is on the table."

"Thanks."

She started to leave but turned back. "You're Chef Jessica, right?"

"I am."

"Ohmygosh, I'm a huge fan. Actually, I interviewed for you, but didn't get the job."

"Oh, I'm sorry. We had so many applicants."

"I understand. No hard feelings at all. I'm just happy to serve you today." She smiled. "Let me know if you have any questions. I'll check back when your friend gets here."

I studied the menu after she left. Their sandwiches looked interesting. I had a few on my menu, but our focus was on more entrée style dinners. After I'd decided on food, I checked my phone again.

Nothing.

Dang it.

Five minutes turned into fifteen, which turned into thirty, and then nearly two hours. I was now using the sugar packets to make little houses and then played a solo game of how many could I stack before they fell.

I messaged him again and again, nothing.

"Do you want to keep waiting or —?" Ashley asked, looking around.

"I think I should go." I was embarrassed and couldn't believe I'd been stood up. I thought he had said he was on his way. "I'll just pay for my drink."

She touched my arm. "Ya know, Chef, it's on me."

"No, I can't do that. I took up your table for two hours. I need to pay something." I took out a twenty, handing it to her. "Keep the change. Thanks."

I stood and walked out without a backward look. That was awful, and I can't believe I sat there that long, but I believed him when he said he was on his way. It was humiliating.

My vision blurred as tears formed in them while I tried to type out a text for Colt. I couldn't believe I sat there for over two hours waiting, but after all the conversations we'd had over the past weeks, I really believed he was interested in me and was a good guy.

Me: I don't know what happened here, but don't call me. I'm done.

Then, I started typing out a text to Vee, but sirens distracted me before I could send it. Flashing lights down the street caught my attention. It looked like something big was happening. A weird bolt of panic shot through my body.

Oh, bleep. I thought.

Looking again at the text messages I'd sent to Colt, they still only showed they had been delivered, never read. I looked down the street. That was towards where he said he lived.

I knew something was wrong. What if he witnessed something and had to stop to give a statement? Or perhaps he had gotten caught on the other side of this and had to wait? So many things came to mind about what had delayed him.

I walked in that direction but got stopped by the police barricades. On the sidewalk was a white covered body, or at least it looked like a body. It was rather large. Staring at it for a moment sent a shiver through my body.

I scanned the crowd for the familiar face of the red-haired teddy bear of a man I'd been conversing with for the past week. No dice. He wasn't standing around or talking with any of the officers.

That's when I saw Detective Upton.

"Detective!" I called out to him.

"Chef? Hey, what are you doing here?"

"I was supposed to have a date, but he didn't show up." I nodded towards the crime scene a few hundred feet away.

"Oh." Then he looked over his shoulder. "Ooh! Um, maybe, but you know I can't tell you anything until we officially identify him."

"I know, but ... it is *a him*?"

"Yes."

"Well, then I guess I wasn't stood up." I frowned fighting the lump forming in my throat.

I stared straight ahead, trying not to look at covered body. If I did, that meant this was real.

"Probably not. I'm very sorry." He looked over his shoulder again, and then back at me. "For what it's worth, you look nice."

"Oh, thanks." I smoothed the shirt a bit, still surprised it fit so well.

One of the other officers called him. He looked at me, simply nodded, then walked away.

I stood there for a moment, taking in the entire scene. This was sad. I can't believe this happened. This isn't what happened, right? I was dreaming. Sure, that's it.

Wake up, wake up, wake up.

But as I walked back up the block towards my car, realization sunk in, and my heart got heavy. Colt was dead.

I didn't know Colt well but knowing he had been killed on his way to see me made this feel personal. A cold chill settled over me as I thought about our last phone call. He had a soothing, deep voice. I could almost hear it now.

The man that on paper looked to be so perfect for me. All we needed to do was meet in person. Now that was gone.

How was I going to tell Noah? Was that even my responsibility?

I got in my car and completely fell apart. Tears streamed down my face as my body shook with grief and unnecessary guilt.

Where do I go from here? I mean, home, but after that. I wiped my tears, staring straight forward for a moment, before finally putting it in gear and heading home.

"What are you doing here?" Vee jumped up when I walked in.

"Colt…" Tears started streaming down my face.

"Oh my gosh, did he stand you up?"

"Sort of." I wiped my face. "I think he was killed or died or something. I don't know. Detective Upton couldn't tell me much, but …" I shrugged. With my messages going unread, him not showing up, and a dead body in front of his apartment building, well it seemed obvious to me.

"What?" Her mouth fell open.

"Yeah. Just my luck, right?" Then I felt an instant guilt thinking something so selfish.

"Oh, Jess! I am so sorry." She hugged me.

After she let me go, I walked into our kitchen, taking a seat at our island. My head dropped to the cool granite top. Without even asking, Vee pulled out a couple of mugs, two tea bags, and began heating some water.

Once the water was hot, she poured the water and then brought the steaming mugs to the island.

"Okay, tell me what happened." Her familiar voice was so soothing.

I told her everything from when I arrived to talking to Detective Upton. Reality was sinking in further and further.

"Oh, Jessie, I'm so sorry. That's awful."

"I feel embarrassed but also guilty."

"I can understand." She hugged me. "I'm so sorry."

My phone chimed. The display showed Noah. Vee and I looked at each other.

"Hey, Noah," I said, answering it.

"Jess, oh my gosh, are you okay?"

"Yes, are you?"

"I don't know. I'm in shock."

"How did you hear?"

"They called his sister and then she called me. We go way back. Dated in high school. She was beside herself, of course."

"Oh, I am sure she is. It is truly awful." I inhaled sharply and exhaled slowly as I fought the lump in my throat. "Do they know what happened?"

"Not much. He was shot as he came out of his building. That's all they know."

My mind imagined the scene. It wasn't hard to do as I saw it with my own eyes.

"I'm sorry for the loss of your friend."

"And I'm sorry about your date. I was a little worried you might be with him when it happened."

"Unfortunately, we never got to meet."

"I'm sorry, but so glad *you* are okay."

We hung up. I stared at the phone. This was all so tragic. I thought after losing my sous chef, Earl, only a few months ago, that I wouldn't go through this again. I hadn't lost many people close to me, unless you count my dad going to prison, which most people don't. Except for great-grandparents that I didn't really know, I hadn't lost any family and only Earl as far as close friends.

But why Colt? Was this tied to me somehow, like Earl had been? I couldn't think of how it could be.

"What did he say?" Vee asked.

"They don't know much about what happened."

"I'm so sorry." She hugged me. "Wanna join Lulu and me for some Netflix?"

"Yeah, let me go change out of these clothes."

"Shame. You looked gorgeous."

"Thanks."

Minutes later, I was snuggled up on the couch next to my best friend and my cat as we watched some new documentary. It was not how I expected to be spending my evening, but it helped to soothe my nerves.

Chapter Two

My night was rough as I kept picturing poor Colt. Dead. Even though I didn't know him, it still broke my heart. He had such a bright energy that came through in his texts and our few phone calls, and now I'd never get to meet him.

While I didn't know his family, I could imagine the shock and pain they must feel right now. I said a silent prayer for them.

The moments I slept, my dreams were full of swirling blood and rain with thunder crashing overhead. I was back to the night my father shot a man. As I watched my father wrestling the gun away from Mr. Jackson, I let out a scream. When the dream version of Mr. Jackson looked over at me, it was Earl's face I saw, a gunshot to his head. That was enough for me to sit right up in bed.

When I was five years old, my father had actually killed a man. He says he was defending me. I hadn't remembered the why until recently. Now I knew the man, Mr. Jackson, had been inappropriate with me.

Mr. Jackson had two children. His son had been three years old at the time of his death and his daughter was born a few months after. Her name was Flora.

She was an artist and I had fallen in love with her work. That was before I knew who she was and what she was up to.

I shook off the nightmare, exhaling as the ghosts of my past fled then pushed myself up.

As I did most mornings, I stared over at Luca. He was an elf portrait that hung on my wall. It was one of Flora's that I'd bought from her a few months ago. Long before I knew her plot with her brother, boyfriend, and her brother's girlfriend, Jenn who had been my assistant manager.

I still loved the painting despite who the artist was.

"Good morning, Luca."

As usual, he didn't reply. Just smiled down with his mischievous grin.

Lulu stretched at the foot of my bed before jumping down and running from my room. I watched her go. She was likely heading to Sawyer's room to climb into his window. He had the best view of the street below and there was a tree that would be full of birds at this time of the day.

I headed to the bathroom and then to my closet. Unlike going on a date, getting dressed for work was simple. T-shirt with my chef's jacket over it with my cargo style chef's pants, then for my hair, I grabbed a red scarf. It highlighted the red stitching in my pants. Okay, so yeah, I put a bit of thought into my outfit, but it was simple.

I was the owner and executive chef, so I liked to look my best, despite being a hot mess by the time the lunch rush was over.

I swiped a touch of lip balm on to protect my lips and then headed out. I'll get coffee at the restaurant today. My mood was to focus on what I could control, and that was cooking. Nothing more.

"Oh, Jessie, are you okay?" Sawyer said when I came downstairs. "I heard about Colt."

"Yeah, I mean, I didn't really know him well."

"Yeah, but still." He didn't have to say what I had been thinking all night.

First Earl and now Colt. Was I bad luck or something? Granted, I'd gone through most of my life with only one other murder hanging over my head, sort of.

If you calculate all the people I have been around since then, it couldn't be me. At least that's what I was telling myself to lessen my guilt.

"So, how was your date?" I asked, trying to change the subject.

"Um, better. We had good conversation. She loves art, history, and video games. We're going to have a virtual gaming date later, so that should be fun. I'll see what kind of a player she is." He laughed.

His quirky dating standards. If they were good game players, they would become more attractive to him. He loved gaming and he wanted them to be part of that with him.

"Well, good luck." I smiled. "I'm off. Have a good one."

Even though it was a Monday, it was a government holiday, so the post office wasn't open. That meant my roommates, who worked at the post office, were likely going to hike or to do yoga, maybe swing through the comic bookstore or the art supply shop. No idea.

I took a detour on my way to work, driving down the block where Colt lives or lived, I guess. My heart thumped at the thought.

Gone. Just gone.

I pulled to the curb near where his body had been covered with a sheet yesterday. There was grayish discoloration on the concrete, but no other sign that anything happened here.

Looking around, the world hadn't stopped. Not sure what I expected to see. Grieving people? A memorial like the one that formed by our dumpster after Earl was shot, maybe?

But no memorial had been started. Cars and people passed by as if nothing had happened. It made me sad. He had been real. He had lived, but now it was almost like nothing happened.

I'm not sure what came over me, but I parked and stepped out of my car and went into the apartment building lobby. It was sparsely decorated with a few dated paintings on the walls, like bad motel art. There was a bulletin board with various advertisements on it. Some were dated from years past.

I guess nobody cleans this thing off.

I turned to face the row of ten mailboxes on the right wall next to a door that read office. It was closed and dark inside. Nothing else to note around here.

I took the stairs in front of me to the third floor and then walked until I saw the crime scene tape. Wait? Crime tape here? Why had they put crime scene tape on his door when he was killed outside? Had they searched his apartment? Was there something dangerous he'd been involved in?

I remember Noah mentioning Colt did some hacking and was a whiz at cybersecurity and IT stuff in general. Could it be related to his death?

As I stood there, the hair on the back of my neck stood up. I looked around for the source of the fear. Nothing, but I had an odd feeling that someone was watching me. It was quiet here, almost too quiet. Unlike when I'd gone to Earl's apartment which had life, crying, yelling, televisions sounds.

Should I leave, or should I try to get into his apartment? Looking down at the lock, I had no idea how to pick a lock, so how I thought I would get inside, I do not know. Even if I could get inside, then what? I'd never been much of a snoop.

Before I could decide what to do, a door two down opened and an elderly lady teetered out. She was pulling a small wire cart with reusable shopping bags in it.

"Oh, deary, are you looking for Colt?"

"Um, yeah, do you know … do you know what happened?" I asked, pointing to the crime scene tape.

"Poor guy was shot last night. Dead in the street. Can you imagine?" She clicked her tongue in disgust. "Were you a friend?"

"Yeah. I hadn't heard from him." I looked at the door and then at her. My words were lies, but the tears in my eyes were real. "I hadn't heard so now, I know. Thank you."

I turned to walk away.

"You work at that new restaurant, right? The Crock Pot?"

"Yes, ma'am. I do."

"Lovely place. My daughter took me there last week for the first time. The pimento cheese reminded me of childhood. My sweet mother used to make something like it for us, but yours is better."

"Well, thank you. I'm glad you enjoyed it." I smiled. "Can I help you with your cart?"

"Oh, that would be lovely, dear. Thank you."

We walked down together, chatting about nothing really, just friendly chit-chat. When we reached the bottom floor, I handed her back her basket.

"Thank you, Chef." she said, patting my arm before heading off in the opposite direction.

I watched her for a moment, then took a glance at the building. I still don't know what I had hoped to find or see, but I guess just to confirm to myself that he was actually gone.

As I was looking up at the building, a curtain moved as if someone had been watching me. That was ridiculous because who would know me here? I looked up the street where the lady had just walked. Other than her, nobody knew me enough to spy on me. It was probably just a coincidence.

I looked up at the window once more before climbing back into my car and headed to the restaurant. I pulled in just as Noah arrived.

"Hey, Jess."

"Hey, Noah. How're you doing this morning?"

His face fell as he let out a heavy breath.

"It was a long night. I talked with his sister again and then with his father, Ralph."

"Do they know anything? Like, maybe what happened?"

"Nothing yet. Frustrating. I'm sure the cops will spend a few weeks analyzing stuff and then throw out this name or that but never come up with the killer."

"Yeah, they were slow with Earl's … um, death." Not sure why the word murder caught in my throat, but I couldn't bring myself to say it out loud.

He nodded as he unlocked the back door for us. We didn't speak about it again after that, as we both got busy with the day.

All morning it felt like I was walking in a fog. My legs were heavy, and every move felt like it took me twice as much energy to do. This was a strange reaction to someone I barely knew.

Like what if he had turned out to be *the one* and now, I'd never know because he was gone? That was a fun, yet sad idea. I looked around, embarrassed and thankful that thought bubbles didn't appear over my head. If anyone knew what was in my head, they would laugh.

The lunch rush had been a perfect distraction and was just what I needed to clear my head. The whole day went by quickly, before I knew it the evening shift was coming in.

"Hey, Chef," June said at three when she came in.

"Hi."

"I heard about your friend. I'm so sorry."

"Oh, well, thanks. He was more Noah's friend, but yeah, it's tragic."

She nodded, then hooked her thumb towards the whiteboard behind us.

"I see soup of the day is potato leek."

"Yep, and it has been selling like crazy. Hannah had to make a second batch for us, but there is still plenty for dinner shift."

"Nice." She walked over to taste it. "Oh, that's good."

"Thanks!"

I gave her the rest of the information about day shift and then headed to the office. Noah and I were the only two managers. We were going to be interviewing for a new assistant to help take some of the burden off of Noah, but that wasn't for a few days.

"Hm, Chef?" Skye, one of the servers, said, sticking her head into the office. "Detective Upton is here for you."

"Oh." I looked at Noah. "Thanks. Tell him I'll be right out."

She nodded and left.

"What do you think he wants?" Noah asked.

"Who the heck knows, but only one way to find out."

I dropped my purse back into the desk and headed to the dining room. I found him leaning against the bar, talking to Ripley with an iced tea in front of him. They were talking about whatever baseball game was on the television behind them.

"Detective," I greeted. I nodded to Ripley, who went into action getting me a peach lemonade. He knew me well. "Thanks."

"Hi, Chef. I'm sorry to drop by, but I was hoping to ask you about Colt Evans."

"Oh, me? What about?"

"We saw that the two of you had been texting and I was hoping to get some information about who else he might have been talking to or who might have targeted him."

"Well, I honestly didn't know him well. We hadn't even met yet in person. Last night was supposed to be a first date."

"So, no idea who he was working with or for?"

"None. We didn't talk about that. Again, we had only just started talking. He is or was friends with Noah, my manager. I hadn't even met him yet, just text messages and a few phone calls. I didn't know him well."

He studied me for a moment. "Okay. I'll make a note. Is Noah here?"

"Um, yeah, I'll get him."

I walked to the back but found that Noah was standing just inside the kitchen.

"He wants to talk to me?" Noah asked.

"Yeah."

"I suppose that was going to happen." He trekked out.

I watched from the doorway but didn't go over. Their body language was unreadable from here, and I had never been good at lip reading.

They wrapped up, and the detective started to walk out, but he saw me and came over.

"I just want to give you a head's up. Chief Stone knows you had been talking to Colt. He wanted me to bring you in for questioning, but I honestly don't believe there is a point."

"Oh, why ... why would I need to be questioned like that?" I knew the answer to that. The chief still had it in for me and my family. My rebellious teen years were never going to let me go, were they?

"You know Stone. He ... um, just likes to cover all bases," Upton said.

"Yeah, I get it," I said, even though I didn't understand. It was twenty plus years ago. People grow and change.

"I'll let you know if we need anything else. Take care."

He turned and strode out of the restaurant. Noah and I stood there in silence, watching him go. We turned towards each other, nodding, then walked to the office.

I grabbed my purse, saying goodnight. I was exhausted and just wanted to get home.

Chapter Three

After I left work, I went home, showered, then face planted on my bed. I just wanted to wallow in the pity of this situation for a moment. I felt bad having my own pity party, given what Colt's family was likely going through. But this was more about how weird my life had gotten, and less about Colt.

The first time in years that I try to put myself out there and the poor guy ends up dead. Logically, I knew I wasn't responsible, but it didn't stop the irrational thoughts from popping into my head.

Lulu jumped up on the bed, pawing at the blankets before settling against my side. I reached my hand out to pet her. She looked at me before moving to the foot of the bed.

What a brat, I thought as I drifted off to sleep.

I was startled awake later by an unknown sound.

"Sorry, did I wake you?" Sawyer asked, standing by the door. He must have knocked, but I wasn't sure.

"Yeah, but it's okay. I didn't mean to fall asleep."

It was a pity party that ended up being a nap, but I kept that part to myself. I rubbed my eyes as I sat up.

"How was work? You okay?"

"Work was busy."

"Staying busy helps," Vee said, coming into the room.

"It does." I smiled at them. "What did y'all get into today?"

"We did some hiking."

"Then we went over to Willowood to the mall. Just did a little window shopping."

"Sounds fun."

"Wanna order pizza and watch TV tonight?" Vee asked.

"That sounds amazing."

Two hours later, we were downstairs. The pizza had been eaten, and we were now watching a new crime drama series Sawyer found. The show was okay, but I couldn't keep my mind on it. I needed something to keep my brain busy or at least busier.

Pulling out my phone, I clicked on the match three game I used to distract myself. It was cheesy, but it passed the time, and I was hoping it would keep my mind off of yesterday, murder, and the police chief who had it in for me.

However, it didn't work. I kept thinking about Detective Upton's warning about the chief wanting me to come in for questioning. Why did he have it out for me? Was it a nearly twenty-year grudge from the time I was a crazy teenager? If so, that seemed insane.

I don't think he had been an officer when my father had killed Mr. Jackson, but maybe he was. If I got a chance, I might ask him. But as far as I know, he wasn't related to him. So again, why did he seem to have it out for me and my family?

Sawyer's phone chimed. He made an almost giggling sound causing Vee and I to exchange an amazed look.

"Is that *your girl*?" I asked.

"Yeah." He flashed a sheepish grin as he typed out a reply.

"They have been texting off and on all day," Vee said.

"Oh, *really*? Well, that's interesting." I sat up. "When do we get to meet her?"

"What? No, not yet." Even in the dim light of the living room, I could see he was blushing. "I am still deciding about her."

"That grin tells me you have already decided," I teased.

"Well, we still haven't played online yet. I need to know if she can keep up first."

"Oh, of course, I forgot your rigorous vetting standards for a girlfriend. So, when does that happen?"

"Later tonight."

"Good luck. I can't wait to meet her." I chuckled.

My phone chimed. It startled me, causing me to fumble with my phone.

"Jumpy?" Vee asked.

"Yeah, apparently." I laughed. "Oh, it's Noah."

N: **Have you checked your email?**

Me: **No, why?**

N: **Colt sent us something.**

Me: **What? How?**

N: **Just check it. Text back after you read it**

"Are you okay?" Vee came to my side.

"Um, yeah, Noah says Colt sent us an email."

"Wow. That's why you look as if you've seen a ghost."

"How is that possible?" Sawyer asked.

"I'm not sure. Noah said just check it."

I pulled up the email app on my phone, scrolling to his email. My stomach churned as it popped on the screen.

Dear Jessica,

If you are reading this, that means they found me. I'm sorry if we didn't get to meet. I was so looking forward to meeting you.

But I was afraid this might happen, so I had set this email to send to you and one to Noah if I didn't enter the password within 24 hours.

I have sent you a passcode in a separate email and provided Noah with a dropbox address.

I hate to put you at risk, but after what you went through for your friend, I know I can count on you to find my killer, too. I haven't put all the pieces together, but the file should get you close.

I didn't want all the data in one place or else they could get it and delete it. I'm hoping that you and Noah can expose the details.

Again, I'm sorry for asking you to do this. It is a lot to ask someone you barely know, but I don't know who I can trust and Noah says you are trustworthy. I saw the lengths you went for your other friend, so I thought you could help me.

I appreciate this. It will give closure to my family and bring these people to justice.

Take care,

Colt

"Holy moly!"

"What?" they asked in unison.

I thrust my phone at them. It was easier that way than trying to explain. Plus, I didn't trust my voice right now. After a moment, they both looked up at me. Their expressions reflected what I was feeling. Confused.

"Wow."

"Whoa."

"Yeah. I have no words," I stammered. A scalding lump sat in my throat, threatening to send tears streaming down my face.

I needed to text Noah back, but I wasn't sure what to say to him yet. I got my phone back.

Me: **Got it. Whoa!**

N: **My thoughts exactly**
Me: **What do we do?**
N: **Chat at work tomorrow?**
Me: **Okay**
N: **You gonna be alright tonight?**
Me: **Yeah. You?**
N: **I think so**
Me: **Ok. Night**
N: **Night**

I pulled up the email again to reread it, then looked for the other email, taking a screenshot of the passcode. Not sure why, but his words that *they* would find it and delete it had me thinking of a back-up way to have the code.

I kept repeating 'they' over and over in my mind. Who were they? Was I in danger now that I had this email? Was Noah?

Oh, bleep, what about Sawyer and Vee?

I looked over at them. I couldn't put them in danger, and this sounded like it was going to be high risk, especially if he wasn't willing to put all the information into one email. I didn't know Colt well, but could he just be a touch dramatic?

No, he was dead, so something had actually happened.

"So, what's your plan?" Vee finally asked.

"Honestly, I don't know. Noah said we can discuss it tomorrow."

"I guess until you know what this file or whatever is, you can't do much."

"Right? Okay, so I should just put it out of my mind."

"Yes."

I got back to my game and tried really hard to focus on it, not the email or Colt or Chief Stone having it out for me. Fail. My mind kept replaying the words in place of the shapes I was supposed to be matching.

It was going to be a long night.

The next day, I cursed at my alarm when it sounded. I had gotten all of fifteen minutes of solid sleep as I tossed and turned and fought the nightmares all night, again. I stretched and looked over at Luca.

"Good morning, Luca."

In my mind, he said good morning in his little elf voice, just like every morning since I bought him. I then went through my morning routine in slow-motion.

I woke up earlier than normal, while everyone else in the house, including Lulu, were all still asleep. Vee and Sawyer should be up any time now to head to work.

Since I wouldn't see them, I wrote a quick note to Vee with a quote of the day. Something we did a few times a week to each other. I looked around once, then headed out to work.

My paranoid brain had me looking left, right, and over my shoulder the entire way. Whoever *they* were could be following me and since we didn't know who *they* were yet, it could be anyone. I pulled into the parking lot, shaking like a leaf, but was relieved to see Noah had just arrived as well.

He was stepping out of his car as I slid into a parking spot next to him.

"Mornin'," he greeted.

"Good morning. You're early, too."

"Yeah, I thought I might as well get a start on the day."

"Were you able to sleep?"

"Not well, but some. You?"

"Same. It's going to be a long day."

"Yeah, so are you ready to look at this stuff?"

"No," I said, causing him to whip his head to look at me. I needed to explain. "I just feel like we are about to open a whole can of worms, but I understand his asking us."

"Yeah, I have no idea what we are about to learn and, to be honest, I'm not really sure I'm ready either."

We unlocked the door and made our way through the kitchen to our office. He booted up the computer and then we waited.

"This thing is slow," I commented.

"Yeah, Colt would probably have been able to fix it for us." He hung his head. "Man, I knew he was into some stuff, but I never thought it was dangerous."

"I'm sorry." I studied him while he logged into his email account. "Did you know much about what he was doing?"

"Not much. I just knew he was a whiz at computers and could hack into computers and systems."

I nodded.

When he had suggested setting me up with a friend, he hadn't told me how close they were. Come to find out, he had dated Colt's sister. He knew his parents, cousins, aunts, and uncles. They went back to elementary school together for crying out loud, but he had mentioned none of that.

I might not have agreed to go had I known. In my experience, if there was heartbreak, it would make my relationship with Noah icky. We had a great working relationship as well as a good friendship.

"Okay, so here is the dropbox. You have the passcode?"

"Yeah," I flashed him the picture on my phone. He typed in the alpha-numeric code.

"It's just a single file." He clicked it. "Another letter? What the heck, Colt?"

To Jess and Noah,

If you are reading this one, that means you have gotten the emails and are together. I hate to do this to you both, but I don't know who I can trust.

Please go to the below address. Use the passcode, but the letters are their placement in the alphabet. A is 1. B is 2, etc.

Be careful.

If my suspicion is right, this needs to get out.

Good luck and thank you both.

Colt

We both looked at each other. This is not what I expected.

"He sure doesn't make this easy or straightforward."

"Yeah, he's always been like this. I think he read too many spy novels as a kid." Noah shrugged.

"So, what is this address?"

Noah typed into the browser. "Looks like one of those mailbox places. This must be a locker combo?"

"I thought those only used like a mailbox key."

"Some of them are like this," he said.

"Shows what I know. How urgent do you think this is?"

"I don't know. We can't go today or tomorrow with all those interviews scheduled. Plus, June is off and without an assistant manager, I can't take off yet either."

I nodded. It was definitely going to have to wait. He printed out the letter and then secured that, along with the passcode, in our safe.

"Best place I can think of," he said.

"Right."

We sat in silence for a moment. Employees started coming in for the day, so we agreed to regroup on this bit of information later. I went to check in with the line cooks and get them started on the soup of the day.

"Tomato and Basil today. I got a nice shipment of tomatoes," I said to Hannah as I pointed to the box of tomatoes.

"They smell amazing." She took a big sniff of them. "I'll get started."

"Good morning, Chef, Hannah," Parker said, coming in. "Chef, I was hoping I could share something with you."

He handed me a container. Opening it, I found biscuits.

"What's this?" I took one out. They smelled amazing. "Is there black pepper in them?"

"Just a pinch, plus a bit of cheddar cheese." His grin told me he had expectations and a lot of hope baked into these biscuits. "Give it a taste."

I took a bit of the tender yet crispy biscuit, moaning as soon as the savory flavor hit my taste buds.

"Wow, these are so good. Are you asking what I think you're asking?"

"Yeah, I was hoping we could add them to the menu. Well, actually, I was thinking when people sit down, they get a basket of them with a little butter and preserves, even though I don't think they need anything added."

"You are so right. They don't need either, but I love the idea." I studied him for a moment. "Okay, let's work out the recipe to make it on a bulk scale and then yes, let's start adding this starting next Sunday."

"Awesome. Thanks so much, Chef." He put his hand out for the container with the remaining biscuits.

"Oh, no, these are mine now." I laughed but held tight to the biscuits.

"Alrighty." He chuckled. "I'm just so glad you like them."

He turned to get to work. He was going to be in charge of the kitchen this morning while I interviewed for the assistant manager position with Noah. Once I was sure he had everything under control, I headed back to the office.

"Here. Try one of these." I held out the container.

He looked at me with a puzzled look but took out a biscuit.

"Oh, my, this is good. What is this?"

"A biscuit."

"No, I know that, but where did it come from?"

"Parker made it. He proposed adding them to the menu. We'll have a complimentary basket of them on each table. Like chips and salsa, but in our case, biscuits with butter and preserves."

"I love it!" He stood, picking up his notebook. "Ready?"

"Yep."

We headed to the dining room to begin the interviews. I hated this part and wished I could leave it to Noah to handle, but given this was for the assistant manager, it was vital that I be involved. I said a little prayer for luck and our sanity.

Chapter Four

It was day two of interviews for our new assistant manager, but we were finally done. If I never interviewed again, I would be a happy woman. However, I knew that wasn't realistic since I owned the business, and it was one of those necessary evils.

This was to replace Jenn after she and her group tried to steal from me and sabotage my business. Their motive was a grudge held by Mr. Jackson's children, Alistair and Flora. The same Flora who painted my favorite elf child picture. Again, that was my father's doing and I had sympathy for them losing their father, so why they went after me, I will never understand.

The four of them were in jail awaiting trial and that's all that mattered now. Well, that and finding a replacement for the assistant manager position.

Noah and I were sitting in the dining room, going through the candidates.

"I liked that last one," I said.

"Me too. Probably the best one."

"Did you intentionally save the best for last?" I joked.

"Ha, maybe. Or maybe we finally got lucky."

Between yesterday and today, we interviewed five candidates. This last one was the only one who really stuck out as a fit. He had the sense of humor we needed and an excellent resume. I wanted to believe it was because he was the right fit, and not just because we were tired of interviewing.

"I'll call some of his previous employers to see what they say, but I'm thinking Cullen could be the one," Noah added.

"He was funny, right?"

"Yeah. More your humor than mine, but I get it."

"Should I be insulted?" I chuckled.

"Hey, take it how you take it." He winked, then made a few notes in his notebook.

I looked down at my blank page. I had never been good at note taking. Maybe I should but I liked to be in the moment, but also sometimes my brain would get stuck on a word, and I'd focus on spelling it rather than listening. Hence, the blank paper.

"That sounds perfect. I'm so glad we are finally done. I hate doing interviews."

"I don't mind them," He said. "But I am glad these are done. Once we get this guy hired and trained, I'll take a day off."

"I've tried to help you."

"Yeah, you've been great and thank goodness for June and Parker being able to work in the kitchen."

"But I know what it was like for me after Earl passed."

I had worked myself to near burnout as I didn't have someone who could work in my place. Earl had been the one trained to fill in for me. Now I had two people who could fill my shoes.

"Yes, I was worried about you burning out. I appreciate your help." He smiled.

We started gathering our things from the dining table when the front door opened. Detective Upton's tall frame filled the door. His ominous presence sent a chill through me. I just knew he came looking for me with bad news.

Please don't be about Chief Stone.

Jordan was on host duty, so she greeted him. He pointed to me without a word to her. That was so out of character for him. My blood ran cold when I realized I must be in some serious trouble with him.

I watched helplessly as he made his way across the room. He was normally an even-tempered, laid-back guy, but the anger seemed to be seething out of his pores as he walked towards me, never breaking eye contact.

Well, bleep, this really can't be good, I thought as I looked at Noah.

"Chef. Noah." Upton greeted us. "Do you have a moment?" He looked straight at me.

"Just me?" I asked.

"Yes, but Noah can stay if you would feel more comfortable."

"Okay. Have a seat." I smiled as Noah and I sat back down. "Would you like a drink or something to eat?"

"Um, no." He frowned and then slowly grinned. "Actually, *can* I get an iced tea and some of that amazing pimento cheese?"

"Yes, of course." I smiled at him sweetly as I waved Ava over and relayed the order. She nodded and went to fill his request. "That will just be a minute. Do you have information for us on Colt?"

"No, but I'm hoping you have some for me."

"Oh? I wish I did." *Bleep*! Did he know about the emails?

"Well, we were reviewing the security cameras at the Beck Apartments and noticed you were there the other day speaking to Imogen Potter."

That must be the sweet lady I spoke to the other day. I hadn't thought to get her name, thinking I'd likely never see her again. Though she knew I owned this restaurant, maybe she'd be in for lunch or dinner sometime.

"I didn't know her name, but yes, I was there. She was pleasant. I helped her down the stairs."

"Yes, well, she was found dead this morning."

My body went numb as tears sprung to my eyes. She had been so sweet, even though I had only met her for a moment. I guess she *wouldn't* be coming in to eat.

"She ... how? What? How?" I fumbled for the words as my mind tried to process what he said.

All these questions popped through my head. Had she died of natural causes, or was she murdered? And worse, was she killed because she spoke to me? Was that why he was here?

But why would someone kill her just for speaking to me? Or was it because she knew Colt? Oh, what if she was involved in whatever got Colt killed?

Noah softly touched my arm. I guess he could tell I was upset.

"I can't give many details, but it appears she may have been killed yesterday."

"Killed or died?"

"Um, killed." He said it just as Ava brought his food.

She quickly looked at me. I half-smiled and nodded my head. She did a slight curtsy as she hurried away. It would be almost a humorous gesture if the situation wasn't so serious.

"I am not sure how I can help. I only had a three-minute conversation while we walked down the stairs together."

"Do I need to point out that you were also an acquaintance of Colt? He was shot and now Ms. Imogen."

"I assure you; I had nothing to do with either of them. You can check the security footage for weeks, months, or longer. I have never been to that apartment building prior to a few days ago."

"And why *were* you there, then?"

"Honestly?" I paused. He nodded. "I was in disbelief about Colt, and I just wanted to, I don't know, see for myself that he was gone. I'm not sure what I hoped to find, but seeing the crime scene tape still on his door made me a believer."

I still had questions about why it was on the door and not the street, but I knew he wouldn't tell me. I'd just keep that question to myself.

He studied me without saying a word. Was he trying to decide if he believed me? I didn't care. I knew the truth. It had been purely innocent. I didn't even try to go into his apartment.

To be fair, if I knew how to pick locks, I might have, but the detective doesn't need to know that. In fact, now that Noah and I had gotten these letters, I really wanted to go snoop around. Again, my lips were sealed.

"Okay, well, knowing you over the past several months, I'm going to believe you. However, you should know that we have a lot of pressure on this one, especially now with two deaths in the same building."

"I get it, but I promise I won't go near it again."

"Well, I didn't say that, just you know the chief," he said softly. He was back to the sweet detective I had gotten to know.

"Yes."

"I don't know what his beef is with you and your family, but he really wants to know what you were doing there."

"As I said, I was just wanting to see for myself. I haven't had the best dating record, and it would just be my luck that he had faked this or that it wasn't him." I tried to laugh, but it came out as more of a groan. Noah gave me a little side eye. "Sorry, Noah. That's insensitive, but you know what I mean?"

"No, I get it."

"Alright, well, that's all I needed." He stood. "Thank you for the iced tea and cheese. Delicious as always."

"I'm glad you liked it. Please let me know if you need anything else. I'm happy to answer your questions." I smiled and walked him to the door.

Once he was gone, I turned to face my employees. A few of them were standing nearby, watching. They likely wanted some kind of explanation. I didn't have one.

"I have no words." I chuckled. "My life is weird."

They awkwardly laughed with me. What can you say to any of this? I went to the office to find Noah.

"Wow, I'm sorry about that," I said, taking a seat.

"Why? You didn't do anything."

"Just that … well, what I said about maybe he wasn't, and you know … all that?"

"Honestly, I get it. I keep hoping the same, but seeing as his funeral is in a few days, I know it's true."

"I'm sorry." I grabbed my purse. "Well, I'm heading out. Call if you need me. Good night."

"Night. Be safe out there."

I nodded, then said my goodbyes to my employees as I made my way through the kitchen. June was back on the evening shift after being off yesterday.

"Night, Chef," she called out as she worked on grilled salmon.

"Night, Chef June," I said to her.

Stepping out into the parking lot, I looked around. I had never been a paranoid soul, but the last several months had me checking around every corner and looking over my shoulder.

The only person visible was a large man standing near the eye doctor's office across the street. He didn't make a move or acknowledge me in any way, so I figured he must be waiting for someone.

Like most days, I arrived at home before my roommates, so I ran up to shower and dressed in more comfortable clothing before they got here. I couldn't wait to tell them about everything that was going on.

An hour later, I was downstairs cooking a simple dinner of spaghetti and meatballs for them when they arrived.

"Honey, I'm home!" Sawyer yelled. He made the same joke every day and every time I laughed as if it was the first time I'd heard it.

"Oh, whatcha makin'?" Vee said, coming to hug me.

"Spaghetti and meatballs."

"Best day ever," Sawyer said. "I'm going to change, back in a few."

"You okay?" Vee asked as she dipped a spoon into the sauce to taste it.

"Is it obvious?"

I knew she could read me better than anyone else. Even Granny and Aunt Rita couldn't read me quite like Genevieve "Vee" Paz.

"You know the answer." She smirked at me.

"Just a long day at work and I got some bad news." I paused. "Why don't you get changed and I'll tell both you and Sawyer together? Then I don't have to tell it twice."

She nodded, hugged me again, and then ran upstairs.

Minutes later, dinner was ready, and my friends came back. We all plated food, then sat at our kitchen table.

"Oh, my gosh, this is so good," Vee said. "I know Sawyer loves your meatloaf, but I think this is my favorite."

"This is probably top five favorites for me." Sawyer chuckled, shoving in a large bite of food. "Okay, tell us about your day."

I sighed. "Where to begin?"

"At the beginning. Y'all were doing interviews, right?" Vee asked.

"Yes, well, we finished the interviews, and we decided on someone."

"Oh, that's good news."

"Yeah, but it went downhill after that when Detective Upton showed up."

"Uh-oh." Vee and Sawyer exchanged a look.

"Remember when I told y'all that I went to Colt's apartment building, and I talked to that nice old lady?"

"Yeah."

"Well, unfortunately, she has died. Killed is what he said." I felt the same gut punch that I felt when Detective Upton told me this afternoon.

"Oh, my gosh. Did he say how or who?"

"No, he doesn't know, but he had questions about why I was there and what I was talking to her about."

"Oh, dang, does he think you are involved?" Sawyer asked.

"That would be insane. You are like the nicest person," Vee added.

"Well, not exactly me, but he wasn't sure if I knew anything. Plus, Chief Stone is on his high horse again about me. I just want to stay out of that guy's way."

"I understand."

"He is the worst."

"So, what do I do y'all? Noah and I haven't had time yet to go to that PO Box, nor will we for at least a week. Not until we get this new assistant manager in place."

"Can you go alone?" Sawyer asked.

"Or could we go with you?"

"Maybe, but I would want to ask Noah first. I would feel disloyal to him. It was his friend, after all."

As it was, I would be filling in as the manager in a few days so he could go to the funeral. June and Parker would be cooking, and I would only be doing manager duties. I wasn't looking forward to it, but I wanted to support my friend as he says goodbye to his friend.

After dinner, Sawyer did clean-up and sent us ladies to relax in front of the television. It was a nice evening despite everything going on.

Chapter Five

Day two of filling in for Noah as the manager. I would be so glad when Cullen started. His references gave him glowing remarks and his background check was perfection. He would start in a week.

Until then, I was the manager and not cooking. Cooking was my passion and it hurt my soul not to cook. Though I tried a few times, June ran me off quickly.

I could only laugh.

Jordan came to the office.

"Chef, a customer would like to speak to you."

"Coming." I stood and followed her to the table. "Hi, how is everything?"

"Not good. Not good at all," The lady said through pinched lips. She reminded me of my fifth-grade teacher. She had a harshness about her that made you want to do your homework and never, ever ask to go to the restroom. "Look at this mush. Is this supposed to be alphabet letters or just mush?"

She poked the soup with her spoon, causing it to break apart. I wanted to argue that stirring and poking it like that would do just that. I could tell by her body language that arguing with her wouldn't help.

"I'm so sorry to hear. We can replace the soup with fresh soup, or you can pick another item." Before I could say I would take the charge off her bill, she interrupted me.

"You think that's going to fix this? I shouldn't have to pay for this."

"Of course. We will be taking this off your ticket. Can we get you anything else?"

"No, I am done. I won't be coming back here." She grabbed the remaining two biscuits from the basket and stomped out.

I stared after her, then slowly turned towards Jordan.

"Wow. Is that normal?"

"I have no idea *what that* was." She snickered and went back to the host stand.

Since I was already out, I made the rounds to other tables. Everyone else had positive feedback, even about the soup. I have a feeling that the lady was not a happy person, but she clearly liked

Parker's biscuits. I didn't blame her. They had only been out two days and people were thrilled by the addition.

After I talked to all the customers, I went back to the kitchen.

"How's everything?" I asked June.

"All good at the moment, but I'm running short on plates. Can you check with Smokes?"

Smokes was our daytime dishwasher. I looked over and didn't see him at the sink or loading the industrial washer.

"Yeah, I'll figure it out." But before I went to find him, I started a load of plates and glasses in the dishwasher, then made my way around the kitchen, storeroom, and then outside. He must be in the restroom, but I couldn't go in there.

Well, if he is in the restroom, it should only be a few minutes. I jumped back to the sink to work on dishes until he returned.

I had everything cleaned by the time he came back. He was a sweaty mess. His skin looked pale, and his eyes looked sunken.

"You okay?"

"No, sorry, Chef. I think I need to head home," he mumbled, but then he turned and ran back in the direction of the restroom.

Okay, so now I am down one employee. Bleep!

I looked around to see who I could shift to this position. Honestly, it was going to be a team effort.

"Marco, I hate to ask this, but can you jump in on dishwashing? Smokes needs to head home."

"Uh, yeah." He clearly didn't want to, and I understood that. He was here to work as a busser.

"I get it, but I really need the help."

"I know, Chef. It's not a problem." He winked and went to take over the dishes from me.

"Thanks. I'll come help out, too."

Hours later, I was wiped out from managing customer complaints and dealing with staff issues. Not that either was overly difficult, especially my staff. They were easy, but it was simply that I wasn't used to doing this.

Most of the time, I had left this side of the business to Noah. Once Cullen started, he would do these types of things.

It did give me a greater appreciation for Noah. He managed a lot that I never saw because I was too busy in the kitchen. I wasn't sure I could do this for a few more days. However, I knew it was important for him to be off to spend time with Colt's family and other friends, so I would suck it up.

I headed home after dark. My mind was on nothing but sleep. As I parked at the curb, it looked like the living room lights were on. Sawyer must be playing one of his games, though normally he kept it dark.

Dragging myself up the few steps, I headed in. My plan was to head straight to the shower and crash face first in my bed.

"Hey, Jess!" Sawyer yelled. "This is Riley."

"Oh, hi," Ambushed by a guest. Exhaustion and the shower had to go to the back burner.

"Hi, Jess. Sawyer has told me so much about you." She came forward.

Was she going to hug me? Only Vee gets away with that without warning and sometimes Sawyer. Never strangers. Never, ever strangers. Thankfully, she extended her hand to shake it.

I took it, giving it a firm shake. It gave me a chance to take her all in. She was shorter than me by several inches. If I had to guess, maybe five feet, six inches. She was blond with green eyes, freckles across her pierced nose. She was wearing a Neal Barney shirt. It was a cat in a jack-o'-lantern.

Jealous. That's a cute one.

"So, what are y'all up to?" I tried to ask cheerfully.

"Just hanging out, playing games," Sawyer said.

"And we had pizza," Riley added, bouncing back over to the couch, and taking my spot.

Hey. Internally, I pouted. *Strike one, Ms. Riley.*

"So, how was work?" Sawyer asked as he continued to push buttons. "Bam!"

I was used to having conversations with Sawyer where he would be in and out due to the game. He often would yell or cheer as we were talking.

"It was okay. Busy. I'll be glad when Noah is back."

"He's the one whose friend just died, right?" Riley asked.

"Yeah."

"That's a shame. Sorry to hear about him and your failed date."

My mouth fell open. Who says stuff like that? I mean it wasn't a failed date. He had been murdered. Huge difference. I was too exhausted to argue or defend myself here.

"Um, thanks." Boy, Sawyer really shared a lot with her. I don't think I liked that.

"Have the police figured anything out?" She continued to probe. "Oh, watch out, babe, zombie on your left!"

He rapidly pushed the buttons. "Thanks!"

"Um, no." I mumbled. I was used to Sawyer being distracted during a conversation, but now there were two of them.

"That's too bad." She frowned.

I stared at her for a second, trying to decide what I thought of her, then I looked at Sawyer. We had been friends for thirty-plus years. She didn't seem like his type. I couldn't figure this out.

"Where is Vee?" I asked.

"She's upstairs reading, I think," Sawyer said. "Oh, take that. sucka!"

Riley cheered.

I had no idea what he was doing in the game. Glad she knew at least. He wanted to date a gamer. Even if she was rubbing me the wrong way, she seemed to make my friend happy.

Lulu came into the room, sniffed in my direction, then hopped up on the couch to sit with Riley. Riley started petting and cooing at her.

Hey, that's my cat. Strike two. I narrowed my eyes at her.

"Well, nice to meet you. I'm beat. Going to head to shower and bed."

"Nice to meet you, too." She waved.

I took the stairs and headed straight to Vee's room, tapping on the door, then opening it. I found her on her bed with headphones on. She saw me and her face lit up.

"Oh, thank gawd you're here." She whipped the headphones off. "Did you meet that awful girl?"

"Yes! What is her deal?"

"I do not know. Came in like she owns the place. She is too … bubbly!"

"This coming from you?"

Vee was the most cheerful person I knew. She rarely gets annoyed with anyone and often found new people interesting, fun, and wanted to know all about them.

"I know!" Vee crossed her arms hard. "Plus, she is only wearing that Neal Barney because of Sawyer. I was asking her questions at dinner. She'd never heard of him before."

"Oh, wow, did she say that?"

"Not exactly."

"Well, I only met her for a second, but she already got two strikes."

Vee laughed. "I missed you this evening. It would have been a lot more fun with you here."

"I'm sorry. Noah will be back in a few days, then Cullen will be starting which means I'll get back to my regular work schedule again soon."

"I'll be glad to have you back here, and not just so you can cook for us."

"I love cooking for you." A huge yawn overtook me for a moment. "Well, I'm going to the shower and hit the bed."

She jumped up to hug me and then waved as she slipped her headphones back on.

I headed to my room, peeling off my clothes, then cranking up the shower. As the hot water heated, I brushed my teeth.

I could hear Riley's high-pitched laughter over the sound of the shower. I rolled my eyes as I hopped in, letting the hot water wash the stress away. It felt so good on my sore, tense muscles.

After I had lathered, rinsed, and repeated, I grabbed a towel to dry off. Looking at my reflection, I looked tired. I touched the bags under my eyes.

"Yikes," I mumbled. Just one more day and Noah would be back.

Lulu came up the stairs as I was dressing. She followed me from the bathroom to my bedroom, hopping onto the bed for some love.

"Well, hello, traitor. Decided to come back to my side?"

She looked up at me and meowed.

"Did she annoy you too?" I started scratching under her chin. She rubbed her head against me, purring loudly, then meowing up at me. "Alright, I forgive you!"

With my cat back on my side, I collapsed for the next six hours.

Chapter Six

A week later, Cullen was starting. I was eager to have him there to help. I got to the restaurant early, as Noah and I were going to meet to discuss the Colt stuff before Cullen got there.

Like most mornings, we arrived at the same time.

"Mornin', Noah."

"Good morning, Jess. Good timing."

"Yeah, almost like we planned it." Technically, we had, but we still laughed at my cheesy joke.

We let ourselves in, turning off the alarm. I breathed a sigh of relief each time I walked in here, and everything was as we left it.

This stems back to when Mr. Jackson's children, Alistair and Flora, and their friends, Jenn and Reggie, had tried to disrupt my business. They had killed Earl, my sous chef, because he'd overheard them talking.

A couple of times during their reign of terror, I found a trashed kitchen. It had been traumatizing. I was so glad they finally caught the four responsible for that drama.

"Are you thinking about Jenn and her little gang?"

"Yeah, I'm so relieved each time I walk into a clean kitchen."

"Me too."

"That left an impression."

"Sure did."

Noah went ahead of me while I flipped on the lights and started a pot of coffee. That was for staff, not the customers. I slept in a little this morning, which left no time for coffee at home. It could not brew fast enough for me. I was ready to stick my face under the drip spout.

"Thanks for holding down the fort while I was out the last few days," he said when I joined him in the office.

"I was happy to. How was the service?"

"It was nice. Colt would have been happy with the turnout."

"There were a lot of people?"

"Yes, though mostly family. Some friends from high school and then others I didn't know."

"Anyone suspicious?"

"Uh, I honestly didn't think about that. Maybe." He rubbed his chin a bit. It looked as if he hadn't shaved in a day or two. He was always clean shaven. "There were a few guys in the back that stood cross armed the entire time."

"I guess you didn't talk to them."

"No, I was too busy comforting April." He slowly grinned.

"Oh, are you?" I didn't have to finish the thought; he knew what I meant. They were starting to date.

"We might be."

"Well, good for you. I'm happy for you. Both of you."

"It's new, so I'm not celebrating. Plus, her brother just died, so it could be a comfort hook-up."

"Hook-up or dating?"

"Dating, I guess. I don't know. It's still new."

"I'm happy for you, whatever it turns into." I smiled. "Okay, so business stuff?"

"Yes, business stuff. Cullen will start today. I have a plan of attack for training him."

"But we are keeping some of the more sensitive things with us, like we did with Jenn."

I had trusted Jenn and she stabbed me in the back. Noah had been right to suspect her. Once he started to suspect her, we took away quite a bit of access to the bank accounts and private information.

"Right. I have his own list of logins and I will be monitoring all vendors, all bank accounts, and all cash transactions."

"Are we being too paranoid?"

"Maybe, but do you want a repeat of what happened before?"

"No, you are right. I don't want that."

I was still nursing some bruises from being batted around when I caught Jenn and her group in the act. I absently touched one of my knees that was still sore. It had been a few weeks now since that happened. Thankfully, most of the spots had healed.

"Alrighty, then we do it this way for now and as we feel we can trust him, we will give him more responsibility."

"Okay, great." I paused. "So, off topic, what are we going to do about that PO Box?"

"I don't think I can take off again for at least a week. Do you think you should go without me? Maybe take Sawyer and Vee just in case."

"I was going to ask you if you would be okay with that."

"Yeah, absolutely. Then once you get whatever it is, we can look at it together."

"Perfect." I stood. "I guess I'll start getting the soups started for the day."

"Sounds good."

With that, our short meeting was over. Gossip, work, and Colt business were all discussed. At my work station, I grabbed my knife and began the prep work for the soups.

I sighed as my blade flew through the onions, celery, carrots. Then I minced up the garlic. It felt so good to be back in the kitchen.

The day zipped by as I settled back in and before I knew it, I was clocking out for the day.

"Hey, so how did your first day go?" I asked Cullen when I went to the office after my shift.

"Well, it's not over yet, but so far, so good. Everyone has been welcoming and helpful."

"Good. I'm glad to hear it." I smiled. "We are happy to have you here."

"Thanks."

"So, before I leave, any questions for me or anything I need to approve?" I posed the last part of the question more to Noah.

He looked at Cullen.

"I don't have any questions, but I am sure I might as I learn more and get more comfortable. Today has been a lot of info at once."

"First days are like that." I laughed.

"And, yeah, I've got nothing for you either," Noah said with a smile.

"Alrighty, well then, I'm going to take it to the house."

"What?" Noah laughed. "Who says that?"

"Oh, is that weird? I think I picked it up from my Aunt Rita. It just means I'm going home."

"If you say so!" He chuckled, and then he and Cullen got back to going over the inventory.

I grabbed my purse and gave a sheepish smile as I left. Walking through the kitchen, I smiled and said good night to the employees I passed. It felt so good to see this all working as it was supposed to. Even more glad that I was leaving while it was still light outside.

Stepping out into the sunshine, I took a moment to bask in the warmth of the sun. Even though it was hot in the kitchen, there was something comforting about a sunny day.

When I got to my car, I sent Sawyer and Vee a text asking if they wanted to go on an adventure later.

S: **Heck yeah!**

V: **Of course**

Me: **Great. See y'all at home.**

An hour later, I was showered, dressed, and was waiting for them to get home. I had the passcode on my phone, but at this point, I had it memorized.

Two-Five-Seven-One-One-Eight-Seven-Three.

"Honey, I'm home!" Sawyer yelled out.

"Welcome home!" I jumped up, greeting them at the door, so glad to have my friend back. No girlfriend today. Thank goodness.

"What's this adventure you promised?" Vee giggled as she hugged me hello.

"Now that Noah's back at work, I got to ask him about the PO Box, and he actually suggested y'all go with me."

"Oh, fun! I'm going to get changed." She ran up the stairs as fast as her little legs would allow her.

"She's so cute." I laughed.

"She is." He looked up the stairs, then lowered his voice. "She had a rough day on the counter, so I'm glad she has this to distract her."

"Oh, no. What happened?"

"She had a few impatient customers. She's such a sweet person, and I know the customers were just frustrated and it wasn't an attack on her, but I hate when she gets yelled at."

"Yeah, I hate to hear that, too."

He smiled and then headed upstairs to change as well.

Thirty minutes later, we were driving over to the mailbox place. Vee was smiling in the backseat. A ray of bright sunshine on a gray day.

I hated that customers took out their bad experiences on her. She was just the face but had no control of lost packages or damaged things.

But even on a bad day, you would never hear her complain. She was so patient and understanding. The epitome of grace and kindness.

"So, what's the plan?" Sawyer asked.

"I don't know yet. I guess once I see what this is, then I can come up with something."

"We should get a giant corkboard and pin all the clues and suspects to it!" Vee chirped.

"What?" I laughed.

"You know how in all the crime shows, the investigator has that board they gather all the clues on. Then they all stand around analyzing it."

"Um, interesting. That might have helped with Earl's murder and all the sabotage."

"I'll look for a corkboard online!" I could hear her tapping on her phone. "Wow, corkboards are expensive. Well, not these small ones, but I think we need a really big one. Those are pushing a hundred dollars or more."

"My dad could probably build us something," Sawyer said. "He should be home on Saturday. I'll ask him."

Sawyer's dad was a truck driver and was gone most weekdays and some weekends. He was hoping to retire in the next few years and set up a custom furniture business. At least that's what Sawyer said about him.

"Oh, here we are, Post and Storage." Vee pointed. "I'm so excited."

"Why?" I turned to look at her.

"It is like we are detectives."

"We are," Sawyer said, as he put the car in park.

"I don't think it counts until we actual solve something," I said.

"You figured out who killed Earl," Vee offered.

"Not exactly. I mean, I was trying, but I just got lucky to catch them in the act."

"But you were close."

Vee was always the optimist. Maybe I could learn from those mistakes and do this investigation better.

We stepped into Post and Storage. There was a customer service desk to the right, with copy machines whirling behind it. There was a space at the back of the shop which appeared to be a computer lab or something. Perhaps for people who didn't have computers?

There was a windowed door leading to a hallway to the larger storage areas, then to the left was a long wall of storage boxes of varying sizes.

Behind the desk were two employees, one had a line of customers while the other was pushing buttons on a machine.

"Hi, welcome!" The button pushing woman said from behind the desk.

We mumbled thanks as we scanned the area.

"So, is this a postal alternative or a storage place?" Vee asked.

"It looks like both?"

"What number is it?" Sawyer whispered.

"Two-eighty-three," I mumbled. I had a right to be here, but I still felt guilty, looking once over my shoulder to see if anyone was watching us. Didn't seem like it? Everyone was just doing what they came to do.

"Ah, here." Vee pointed.

It was one of the smallest ones. It was about the size of an average shoe box. It couldn't hold much, so what did it have inside?

I punched in the number, and the lock clicked. I pulled the door open. Inside was a brown paper envelope.

I looked at my friends, unsure about taking it. Something about this set the hairs on the back of my neck on edge. It was almost like life's secrets were about to be revealed.

Taking a deep breath, I pulled the envelope out. I expected it to have paper in it, but it felt like there was something small and light weight inside.

"What is it?" Vee softly giggled.

"I don't know." I shook it lightly. "Let's get out of here and open it at home."

I relocked the door on the box, then calmly walked out as if I hadn't just stolen something. In fairness, I didn't. The owner had given me instructions to come get it, including the code, but it still felt kind of wrong.

Back in the car, we all let out a tense laugh.

"Straight home, or do we want to stop for dinner somewhere?" Sawyer asked.

"I could eat," Vee said.

"Me too."

"Alrighty, Beaks and Brew or Polly's Pizzeria?"

"Oh, tough choices," I said.

"Polly's!" Vee yelled.

We all laughed. Sawyer put it in gear, and we headed to Polly's. I tucked the envelope safely into the bottom of my purse. It would be safe there through dinner, I hoped.

As we were pulling out of the parking lot, I noticed a large man standing staring at us. Was that the same man that was outside of the eye doctor the other day or was I going a little crazy?

I rubbed my eyes and looked again, but he was gone. Ugh, I was one paranoid person these days.

Chapter Seven

After dinner, we went to the comic bookstore to browse around. Vee went straight to the figurines to see if there were any new ones, even though she had an alert set up for when new ones came out. Sawyer went to the comics while I went to the back wall to see what local art they had for sale.

I was sad that there was no longer any new Flora artwork, what with her being in jail and all. I had really wanted a sibling or friend for my Luca. Until I found a new artist that could paint like her, he was going to remain solo.

I walked the length. A few dragons that might be good friends to Luca. There were wizards and unicorns, a troll. A set of four canvases with mushrooms was interesting, but not exactly my style.

"Anything catch your eye?" Monte asked when I went to stand by the register.

"Nay, not today. Though I liked the Wayne Carter one."

"Yeah, he is a new artist. Up and coming. He's promised some new things next week."

"Well, I'll try to come back next week to check it out."

My friends finished up. Vee bought a new figurine and Sawyer bought a new indie comic.

"Thanks, kids," Monte said.

"Bye, Monte."

"Thanks."

"See ya next time."

With that, we walked out into the parking lot.

"Y'all ready to go home?" Sawyer asked.

"Yeah."

"Unless you want ice cream before we head home," I suggested. I think I was stalling. I didn't want to see what was in that envelope. Even though I was curious, I was nervous about finding the next clue. Discovering who they were could put me in danger.

"I could eat some ice cream," Sawyer said with a laugh.

"Me too."

We walked through the parking lot to We Scream Ice Cream. It was all homemade, with specialty flavors. Just like everything in this town, it was an artisanal creation.

We all ordered a different flavor so we could share a little bit of each. They were all so good. I could never pick my favorite.

"Well, I'm ready to get home now," Sawyer said, patting his stomach. "I have a date with Riley."

"A date or an online date?" I really didn't want to see that girl.

"Online."

"Well, enjoy." I looked over at Vee, who was shoveling ice cream into her mouth. It was her way of avoiding adding to the conversation.

When we got home, Sawyer left us to head upstairs to get changed and ready for his date. He would be back shortly, as the gaming system was in the living room.

I set my purse down and dug the envelope out of the bottom, testing the weight in my hand.

"Well, what do you think?" Vee asked, putting her arm around me.

"I don't know. I'm oddly nervous about it."

"It's understandable. This might tell you who killed him."

"I still don't understand why he got me involved in this. I barely knew him." A lump formed in my throat as my mind thought of what might have been. No sense going there again.

"Because you are a wonderful and an amazing person."

"Of course you'd say that, but he didn't know me well."

"He must have had a good instinct."

"Not good enough since someone killed him." I frowned.

She didn't say anything. What could you say? She simply hugged me a little tighter and then went to heat up some water to make hot tea for us. It was her go-to when someone needed to be comforted. She once said it was what her grandmother would do.

I followed her to the kitchen, taking a seat at the kitchen island. I put the envelope down. Why was I hesitating?

"Like a band-aid, right?" I chuckled and then ripped the tab. Tipping the envelope, a USB drive fell into my hand. "Dang. I knew it was going to be just another wild goose chase."

I took a picture and sent it to Noah.

"So, just another USB?" Vee asked.

"Yeah, I guess now I have to see what is on this one." I laid it on the granite top of our island, spinning it. I had no plan to do it at this moment. In fact, I might wait to look at it with Noah.

"What was in the envelope?" Sawyer called out as he came bouncing down the stairs.

"Another USB drive."

"Seriously? That guy didn't make things easy."

"Not at all, but whatever the information he got into was enough to get him killed, so it is worth hiding." I shrugged.

Vee placed a mug of tea in front of me. I wrapped my hands around the warm mug. It felt so good and grounding.

My phone chimed.

N: **Bring it tomorrow and we can look at it together?**

Me: **Yeah, that's what I was thinking too**

N: **Great. See ya bright and early**

Me: **Yep. BTW, how are things going there?**

N: **Cullen is great. I can't wait for a true day off**

Me: **Good and soon!**

N: **Night**

Me: **Good night**

Sawyer hugged me and then went to start his online gaming date. Vee and I stayed in the kitchen drinking our tea. She started to tell me about this person or that. Gossip she picks up at the post office. I listened and did all the right responses, but my mind was on Colt and the latest USB.

Dang it, Colt. I know I didn't know you well, but could you have made this any more difficult?

I really hoped this had the information we needed to take to the police, and I hoped it didn't get us killed in the process. After this, I hope I'm never involved in another murder investigation again. I loved cooking. I was not a sleuth.

"Did you hear me, Jess?" Vee said.

"Oh, I'm sorry. I think I zoned out for a moment."

"I asked if you wanted to go watch-listen in on Sawyer's date." She pointed towards the living room.

"Well, while I am not a fan of Riley, I do love watching him."

We giggled and took our drinks into the living room. He had a weird grin on his face. Vee and I exchanged a smug look.

He was quieter than normal, which had me oddly intrigued in watching him. He didn't seem to notice we'd come in the room, but when he noticed, he simply grinned and then focused on whatever in the game. Clearly, this Riley was doing well at game night and on our guy. I might not like her, but she was making him happy, so for that I could put up with her.

In the past, he had tried to rope me into playing. I just randomly hit buttons and hoped for the best. Usually, I ended up going the wrong way and then getting stuck in a corner of a building or something.

"Oh, good one, Riley!" He shouted after a few minutes.

Vee and I smirked at each other.

We watched our friend for another hour, before I got bored and said good night. I was surprisingly tired, and I had a big day tomorrow.

Chapter Eight

I slept like a baby. Now I was ready to face the day and whatever was on that USB drive of Colt's. After drinking a cup of coffee at home, I dressed and headed over a little early.

The streets of Dashwood were hopping at eight am as I headed in. We didn't have much of a rush hour like the larger cities, but for our area it was traffic. I had to wait through two light cycles before I could cross to the restaurant.

I laughed at myself at the thought.

Two whole light cycles.

Having been to other cities, it was sometimes much heavier traffic and waiting only a couple of minutes to arrive was nothing. Once, I was nearly late to a competition in New York City because of underestimating the traffic. I should have given myself an extra twenty minutes, at least.

I pulled into the empty lot.

Once I was inside, I went straight to the office to boot up the computer. Then, while our ancient machine came to life, I went to make the coffee and start prepping for the day. At least until Noah got here, so we could go through whatever Colt left us.

"Mornin', Chef." Arlo, my maintenance man for the restaurant, greeted me as he came in.

He headed straight to the storage closet to gather supplies. He fixed broken things, kept the plumbing working, and did all the exterior cleaning. I hadn't originally thought of hiring a maintenance person, but Noah had suggested it right before we'd opened.

Arlo had been such a smart hire. Not only his work ethic and personality, but he could fix anything and didn't mind the dirty jobs.

"Off to clean windows," he called as he headed outside.

Before the back door closed, in walked Noah.

"Hey, Jess. You're early."

"Uh, I thought we agreed to be early."

"Yeah, we did. I was just sayin' ... small talk." He shrugged. "Do you have the drive?"

"I do. I left it in the office."

"Great. Did you look at it yet?"

"Not yet. I wanted to wait for you. I mean, you knew him better." I paused. "I'm just helping."

That was all true. I had no idea why he wanted me involved. He said because I solved Earl's case, but technically I didn't.

"Well, let's go look."

He sat at the computer while I took the chair next to him. He stuck the USB into the slot, clicking around until a folder opened.

"This has over two thousand files in it. Wow!" He whistled.

"Really?" I leaned forward to look. The files didn't have names, just random numbers. "What do you think the numbers mean?"

"No, idea. They almost seem like generic default names."

"You don't think they are dates or something?" I grabbed a piece of paper, writing a few down to see if I could figure out a date or a pattern. "Never mind. Must be random."

"Which one should we start with?"

"I guess the first one."

He clicked the file, and a grainy picture popped up.

"Oh, are these all pictures?" He scrolled to the top, changing the view from list to icons. It showed that more than half were pictures, but it looked like there were files mixed in. We clicked through a few that showed more grainy, hard to see pictures.

"This isn't much to go on." I sat back, but then, as he clicked on the next picture, I sprang forward. "Wait stop! No, go back one."

"Oh, my gosh, is that—?" He asked.

"It does look like him." I stared.

He is the Finance Director of the city, but I didn't know much about him. However, if I had to guess, it was something shady with the money and likely the city's money. It was like a predictable movie, but worse because I couldn't guess what was going to happen next.

"Is that Chief Stone with him?" Noah blurted, pointing at the next picture.

"Maybe. Hard to tell. Click a few more."

He nodded and clicked through a few more before we had a clear enough picture.

"Yep, it is Chief Stone with Davis Campbell."

"Well, that can't be good." I sat back. "What could they be doing?"

"Your guess is as good as mine." He rubbed his hands through his hair, muttering. "Colt, man, what were you into?"

"If he died because of this, it had to be big, like maybe millions of things he was into or at least had some knowledge about."

He looked at me with tears in his eyes. Seeing that shook me to my core. His typical take charge, no nonsense attitude was what I liked about him. Tears didn't bode well for that normal Noah vibe.

"Are you okay?"

I started to reach for his hand, but then stopped myself. He wasn't the touchy-feely kind, but neither was I. At least normally but seeing my friend and manager hurting had me wanting to comfort him.

"No, honestly, no. He was like a brother to me. Heck, I thought I would be his brother-in-law one day. Now, even if April and I do get married, Colt is gone. Just gone."

He reached for my hand as tears fell from his eyes. We sat crying quietly together, holding hands. My tears were for his pain and for his tears. It broke my heart to see him in so much pain.

We stayed like that in silence, tears falling until we heard Arlo come back inside. Noah passed me a tissue, then took one for himself.

"Thanks." He mumbled. "Not many people I could cry with and not be embarrassed."

"Well, I'm here for you, and if you need to take more time off, we have Cullen now. Plus, Parker and June can easily run the kitchen so I could work with him," I said, standing to leave.

"Thanks, but no. I think I need to work. It will be a good distraction."

That's how I always felt, too. Work until I drop and forget my problems and stressors. Maybe why we worked so well together.

"Okay. Just let me know if you need anything. I'm going to get to work. Soup isn't going to cook itself."

He chuckled softly, wiped his face, then turned to the computer.

Hours later, June was in for the night. It had been a busy day. I loved these days. They went by in a blink, and I got to cook food for hours. Best day ever.

"Hey, guys. How's day two going?"

"Great!" Cullen grinned. "Noah is a great teacher."

"He's a quicker learner," Noah added.

"Well, wonderful." I reached in the desk for my purse. "I'm heading out. Night, y'all."

"Wait up, Jess. I'm going to walk you out," Noah said. "You good for a few?"

"Yeah, yeah, of course."

"Just come get me if you need me, but I should just be a minute." he told Cullen.

We headed out to my car.

"So, April called me earlier. She needs to clean out Colt's apartment, and asked if I could help."

"Oh, wow, I assume you said yes."

"Of course, but I wanted to see if you wanted to help and maybe Sawyer and Vee?"

"Why us?"

He looked around. I followed his scan, not seeing anyone. "I was thinking it would be a good chance to look around and see if we could find clues."

"Ah, yeah. That makes sense, but why Sawyer and Vee?"

"We'll need extra hands. Plus, Vee talks a lot. She can keep April busy while we look."

"Ah, yes. Okay, just let me know when."

"I told her we could do Sunday. Cullen should be up and running, plus you're off."

"Okay, we'll be there. Text me the address." I started to get in my car. "No, wait, I know where it is. What time?"

Not sure where my brain was these days. The only time I felt like myself was when I was cooking.

"9 a.m."

"Perfect." I clicked the key fob, unlocking the doors. "Oh, and Vee had a crazy idea that I'm starting to think isn't so crazy."

"Oh, boy, can't wait to hear this one."

"Yeah, just wait. She suggested we make one of those investigation boards, clue boards, whatever they are called like you see in movies."

"And tack the clues to it! Brilliant. I think we should."

"Great! We'll have to do it."

"Let me know. I'll come over to help set it up."

"Maybe after we go through Colt's apartment. Hopefully, we will have more clues then," I said.

"That's a good plan."

"So sometime after Sunday."

"That works."

We waved to each other as I climbed in my car, and he headed back inside.

Now I would just need to ask Sawyer and Vee. I knew they would agree to it. They loved to help others, especially as a favor to me. Noah wasn't wrong about Vee. Her gift of gab would be a great distraction.

Chapter Nine

When the alarm went off at seven on Sunday, I groaned. Why had I agreed to this? Well, not the helping part, but the early hour on my day off. Oh well, I was helping a friend and also snooping a bit.

I stretched, looking around for Lulu. She must be in Sawyer's room, or maybe she was downstairs. Who knows? She had an active life here in our townhouse with only one room being off limits to her, Vee's room.

I climbed out of bed, heading straight to the bathroom. My hair was going in three directions.

"Beautiful," I mumbled as I tried to tame it with my hands.

Once I was done in the bathroom, I headed downstairs for coffee and maybe a quick breakfast. I found Lulu coming into my room as I was going out.

"Well, good morning, Lulu kitty." I reached down to pet her. She rubbed against me, meowing. "Did you have a good night?"

She meowed.

"Oh, did you sleep with Sawyer?"

"Yes, she did. Right on top of me." He chuckled as he came out of his room. "Remind me why we're up so early?"

"Ha, really? I was thinking the same," I said, as we arrived in the kitchen, grabbing mugs and heading to the coffeepot. "I think we have some bacon. I can make us some breakfast."

"Oh, yes, and could you do those hash browns with the onions and peppers in it?"

"Let me check for peppers, but yeah, I can make that."

I sipped my coffee, then started digging for ingredients. Sawyer sat at the island to watch me work.

"Watching you dice onions and shred potatoes has always been my favorite thing. It is so mesmerizing."

"Thanks." I said as the knife flew through the onion, then the red pepper.

"Good morning, family," Vee said, finally joining us. "What smells so good?"

"She's making those potatoes with the onion and peppers."

"Oh, and bacon?"

"Yep, it's in the oven," I said, stirring the potatoes. "Coffee's ready."

"Yay!" She grabbed a mug, added a splash of her vanilla creamer, before taking a seat next to Sawyer. "I'm excited about today."

"You are?" Sawyer looked at her. "I'm dreading it a bit. How weird is it to clean up a dead man's apartment, especially one we didn't know?"

"Good point." She laughed nervously. "I shouldn't be excited."

"No, you feel how you want. I know you love meeting new people. April is new to us." I smiled at her. "Okay, breakfast is ready."

I grabbed plates, piled each with food then placed them in front of each of my friends. I leaned against the counter across from the island to eat. Conversation was limited to things like this is good, pass me the jam, and thank you.

"Okay, I got cleanup," Sawyer said, jumping up.

"Thanks. I'm going to get ready. Meet down here once we're ready?"

They both nodded. Vee and I went upstairs to get dressed.

At about quarter to nine, we climbed in the car to head over to Colt's. It was a short drive to his place. Parking was hard to find. The closer spots were reserved for residents, but we managed to find a spot near the end of the block.

I guess I'd gotten lucky the day I met Imogen Potter. People would have been at work then.

"Is that Noah's car?" Vee pointed.

"Oh, yeah, looks like it."

"How's he doing with this?"

I wasn't sure if I should share that we cried together the other day, so I simply said he was doing okay.

"I would be devastated if something happened to either of you," Vee said. She hooked her arms into ours as we walked to Colt's building.

Stepping inside, I could picture poor Ms. Imogen Potter. She was potentially killed just for talking to me, but of course, we didn't know the true reason she was killed. But for what other reason could she have been murdered?

As we walked up to his floor, I looked around at each door, each shadow, and listened for any noise. Who had done it? The people in 2A, perhaps? There were a lot of strange sounds behind their door. Perhaps that was just the television.

"Sounds a lot like Call of Duty," Sawyer said, looking over at the door.

"Ah."

I guess I wasn't the only one paying attention to the sounds of the building. I, again, couldn't help but compare things to last time I was here. It was quieter then, but now it was like any other noisy apartment complex.

Makes sense as previously, it was a workday and this was the weekend. More people would be home.

We made it to the third floor and saw that Colt's door was ajar. My heart thumped rapidly as we got closer, but then I heard soft voices from inside. One was Noah's. I let out a sigh of relief.

"Knock, knock," I said at the door but didn't step inside.

"Come in," a female voice called.

I pushed the door open. In front of us was the living room with a pile of boxes, a couple of rolls of tape, and Noah with a beautiful redhead. She was more of the girl next door beauty, not the model on TV kind. I actually preferred that look, and it was clear that Noah did as well.

"Hey, guys, this is April Evans," Noah said. "April, this is Jess, Sawyer, and Vee."

"Hi, nice to meet you all." She shook our hands. "Thank you all for coming to help us. As you can see, there is a lot to pack up."

Following her motion, I finally got to fully take in the room. Half of the living room had simple furnishings of a sofa, a side table, and a television on the wall. Across from there was the dinette that Colt had set up like a computer room.

The focal point was a large U-shaped desk with six flat screen monitors attached by arms to the desk. Then there was a computer, mechanical keyboard, and a joystick style mouse. There were drawers cocked open to reveal what looked like random office supplies and an open notebook with a pen on top.

"So, where would you like us to start?" I offered.

"We were just trying to figure that out." Noah smiled. "We were taping up boxes, so we were be ready to load them all up."

"I don't even know what I'm going to do with all this stuff," April said. "My parents don't want it, but I can't just throw it all out."

"You could donate it?" Vee offered. "There is a place on West that helps single parents. That's where I always take stuff."

"That's a good idea. I'll call them." April smiled, pulling out her phone. "What's the name?"

Vee helped her find the number, and they went into the kitchen to make the call. I turned to Noah.

"What should I do?" I whispered.

"I think the desk has files in it and maybe there are more USB drives. I'll see if I can get her to start in the bedroom, which will give you a chance to look."

"And what should I do? I want to help with this, too," Sawyer said.

"Um, oh, maybe you can work in the kitchen and then use some kind of keyword to tell her if April is coming."

"Okay, good plan."

April and Vee came back into the room.

"Alrighty, they said they could take most of it. Then we called a secondhand clothing store about his clothes. The rest will just go into the trash. Like all the old food, household cleaners, and partially used toiletries." She touched Vee's arm. "Thanks for getting me organized. I have been dreading this for a week now."

"Well, while y'all did that, we broke up some of the jobs. You and I can start working in his room, Sawyer and Vee can do the kitchen, and Jess will start working out here. Perhaps with the desk area?" Noah said, catching my eye.

"Oh, wow, the desk." She clapped her hands, turning to look at it. "Yeah, that would be helpful. All those shelves and equipment. Those I'll probably take with me." She turned to Noah. "But you might want some of his things, pictures and such, right?"

"Yeah, Jess, just use your best judgment. We trust you," Noah said, giving me a wink.

"Great. I'll be sure to label the boxes accordingly."

I guess we didn't need a secret word between me and Sawyer any longer. April seemed okay with our plan. That was a relief because I could snoop a bit without looking suspicious.

With that, we broke up into our groups armed with trash bags, boxes, and black permanent markers.

I stared at the desk for a moment. I could almost picture him sitting there, though I'd only seen two pictures of him. His red hair cut short, his green eyes sparkling, and his freckled nose was hard to forget. It was a shame that we never got to meet.

I shook out one of the trash bags and set out a box. I grabbed some of the random office supplies, throwing the pens, paperclips, and other items straight into the trash. Then I found a stack of notebooks. Flipping them open, a few were blank, so I threw those away. The others, I put in a box. I wrote Noah on it. I set up a second box with April on it.

I began going through the drawers, getting rid of some stuff, putting some in Noah's box, and keeping a few personal items for April's box. When I got to a picture of Colt and April together, I took a moment to stare at it. They had the same eyes and smiles.

Then I found a small organizer full of USB drives.

"Dang," I mumbled to myself. There was no way to tell if they had anything on them or not. I put the whole container into Noah's box. We could go through it all later.

After an hour, I had everything boxed or trashed from the desk, including unhooking the computer and monitors. I wrapped them in some stretch wrap that they had, so they were secure for April to transport.

"Hi, April," I heard Sawyer say a little loudly.

She laughed as she said hi back. I guess he was just being extra careful that I wasn't doing something shady.

She came into the living room, picking up a roll of tape.

"Hey, you got it all done." She smiled. "It looks good. Thank you."

"Not a problem."

"Between me and you, I was worried about what my brother had gotten himself into."

"Oh?"

"Yeah, my dad thinks he was doing some illegal stuff. I wouldn't be surprised. I mean he was freaking killed in the street."

I thought about what she said. If he had been killed, why hadn't the killer come to his apartment? Why was this all still intact?

Looking over at the door locks gave me at least one clue. There were four locks on the door. It's possible the bad guy couldn't get in.

"I'm sorry."

She flashed a weak smile.

"We could use some help back here if you're done," she offered.

"Alrighty."

I grabbed a few extra boxes and followed her to the bedroom. It was a strange feeling as I stepped into Colt's bedroom. I'm sure it now looks very different from when he was last here.

What had he thought that morning? Was he just as nervous-excited about our date? Had he taken time to pick an outfit, like I had? Probably not, but it was still funny to think about.

"We almost have his clothes packed." April smiled, tears in the corner of her eyes. She picked up a bag from the ground, handing it to me. "Noah said you like Neal Barney. He was Colt's favorite, too. These were his, and I thought you might like them."

I took the bag, opening it slightly, I could see at least five t-shirts with the telltale Neal Barney look to them.

"Thanks" A lump formed in my throat.

It sounds like we *really* did have a lot in common, especially when I saw the artwork lining his walls. He also liked elves and dragons. I didn't currently have dragons on my walls, but I did have a few figurines on my dresser.

April caught my stare.

"Do you like any of them?"

"Oh, um, they're nice."

"Take any you want. They will be getting donated or trashed otherwise."

"Maybe." I eyed one of the elves. It would go perfectly with Luca, but then I saw a dragon that I liked a bit better. "Could I take this one?"

"Of course! Knowing Colt, he would probably like you to have it." She smiled.

"Thank you."

I took it off the wall and put it along with the bag of t-shirts to the side, then started working with them on cleaning out the bedroom. Nothing of interest here, just normal bedroom stuff.

Hours later, the Nearly New Shop had swung by to pick up the large furniture and all the kitchen items. April and Noah loaded his clothing into her car, and the boxes they were keeping into his. Sawyer, Vee, and I took out the trash bags while they did that.

As we were heading back, I was daydreaming about what could have been when I bumped into a man. He was larger than me, not only tall but wide.

"Oh, I'm sorry," I said.

"You should watch your back. You don't know what you've gotten yourself into," He growled, then quickly walked out the back door of the building, disappearing from my sight.

I was too stunned to react quickly enough to ask him what he meant or get a good look at him. I turned around to see where my friends were. They had gone up one flight of stairs, but paused to see where I was.

Was it my imagination or was that the same guy that I'd seen standing by Dr. Vega's eye clinic and then again outside of Post and Storage? It couldn't be. Could it?

"Jess, you okay?" Vee looked down at me.

"Um, I … Yeah, coming."

"You're as white as a ghost," Vee asked when I caught up. "Are you sure you're okay?"

"I bumped into a man, but now I'm wondering if he actually ran into me on purpose. He threatened me."

"Where? What man?" Sawyer growled, running back down the stairs. "Which way, Jessie?"

"Out the back, but please don't follow him, please. I don't need two dead friends," I begged.

"Let me just peek out the back. I won't follow."

He disappeared from sight as he walked towards the back door. I could hear his steps move away and then back.

"All clear. Damn."

"What were you going to do if you saw someone?"

"I don't know. Ninja stuff."

Vee and I exchanged amused looks. He always wanted to be our protector, and to date, he had done well. Mostly verbally, nothing really physical. Except once on a trip to New York City for a cooking competition. Some guy grabbed Vee. Sawyer punched him. The guy hit the floor.

Thankfully, no charges were pressed since we had witnesses that the guy had assaulted her first. But it had been a stressful situation.

April and Noah rejoined us in the apartment. We all did a quick once over around to make sure everything was picked up. I grabbed the bag of t-shirts and the elf portrait before we all trudged back down the stairs.

"I put that one box in your car like we talked about," Noah whispered when he was away from April.

It was the box of paper files and USB drives from Colt's desk. Noah wanted me to go through it. He said he and April were together a lot now, and he didn't want her to see it. Made sense to me.

"Okay, I'll let you know what I find."

They went one way while us three misfits went the other.

"I'm glad we helped. April really seemed overwhelmed." Vee said.

Yeah, plus I had a huge box to sort through, but I didn't say that out loud.

"Did you know that Colt was into Neal Barney?" Sawyer asked. "Just like Riley."

"No, I guess we would have talked about it at some point, but we didn't have the chance." I ignored his comment about Riley as tears formed in my eyes.

I looked out the window, not wanting to think about the what ifs. I played that game enough over the last few weeks. Now whatever and whoever Colt was, was now in boxes or the trash. It was like he had never existed, except he did. It made my heart hurt a little to think that.

Chapter Ten

We grabbed dinner on our way home. Take out from Sushi 73 and then came home to sort through the box of stuff. Vee volunteered to check out the USB drives. Sawyer and I were going through the paper files.

Most were boring personal things, like copies of his taxes or receipts for car repairs. Nothing connected to Finance Director Campbell or Chief Stone.

"Hand me that other USB. This one is blank, too," Vee asked as she pulled it out of her laptop.

"Here, take the entire box." I passed it to her.

"Thanks." She grabbed one and stuck it into her machine.

"There isn't much here. Why didn't you give this stuff to his sister?" Sawyer asked.

"Well, I didn't sort through the files there. Just grabbed and stuffed them in the box."

"Fair enough," he nodded, going through the next folder.

"Since he had all the other stuff on that USB from the storage place, do you think he would have kept any of it at home?" Vee asked, placing another drive into the computer.

"I don't know. This was Noah's idea, but he is with April right now and doesn't want her to know what's going on."

"Yeah, she's sweet. I like her," Vee said. "It's a shame what happened."

I nodded and started looking through the next folder. This seemed to be personal emails and memes he printed. I looked at each, laughing a little at a few. There were lots of superhero and comic ones which I liked, too. We do have the same sense of humor.

I shuffled a few more and found a collage of pictures of him with Noah. Their smiles showed years of friendship, mischief, and memories. Text across it read "happy birthday, Colt."

I had to assume it was from Noah.

"I think I got something," Sawyer said. "Look at this."

I took the pages from him. They looked like financial records. They weren't in order, so I shuffled them around until I found the first page.

"J.W. Dashwood Fine Arts High School," I muttered.

"As in—?" Vee leaned over.

"Yeah, as in my high school."

The school wasn't just fine arts any longer, but when it started, it was focused on visual arts, performing arts, and design. Then twenty-five years ago, they added the culinary arts program, and I was one of the first classes. Five years or so after adding culinary arts, they added cosmetology and barber certification classes.

I tried to read through what each item was, but it just looked like the school's budget for last year. Noah would know more about what all the accounting codes meant. I knew a little just from being in business, but he had more detailed training on this.

"Do these charges add up?" Sawyer pointed. I could see his lips moving slightly. He was likely doing the math in his head.

We often called him the human calculator. He could take almost any numbers or math problem and solve it in his head. "Yeah, it looks like something is missing from these subtotals. By about a hundred here, two hundred here, and um, ten carrying the two, another hundred here. Just a few small amounts across several items, but where are they putting that?"

"That's weird."

"Here, let me look at them again." He took the pages back, flipping through them.

I stared at him in awe. He was amazingly smart and could do much more than load boxes and packages all day, but he loved what he did for a living. I could completely understand that as well. The whole if you love what you do, you never work a day in your life thinking. He was one of the happiest people I knew and that made me so happy for my friend.

"Why are you looking at me like that?" Sawyer chuckled.

"I just love you, my friend."

"Ha, love you, too, goofy." He patted my hand. "So, look at this. It appears like someone moved funds from the culinary arts department out to an external bank."

"You don't think Mr. Jones did that?" Vee asked.

"No way. No way, I can't believe that," I said.

"No, of course not. He is a good guy," Sawyer said. "Let's keep looking."

He put those papers in a separate pile, and we began digging again, while Vee continued with the USBs. We got to the bottom of the box without finding anything else.

"Well, dang, we got at least a clue. Maybe I need to sort through the files on that USB from the storage place better."

"I can help," Vee offered.

"I'd love to stay and help, but I got a date." He stretched, then stood up.

"Ah, out or online?"

"Out. We are going to see the Trash Pandas."

They were a local band. I had seen them once before. They put on a fun show.

"Well, have fun."

We watched him go.

"I'm happy for him." I smiled. "Even if I don't care for her."

"Me too." She smiled. "Want me to start us some tea?"

"Yeah. Should we move over to the island to go through this stuff?"

"Yep." She grabbed her laptop, and I pulled the USB from the PO Box out of my pocket.

She started some hot water and set up our mugs while I plugged in this drive. I sorted the files by the type. I didn't think I needed to go through the pictures again. Instead, I wanted to focus on what the files held.

I opened the first spreadsheet. It was more financial records, but these weren't as clear cut. I couldn't see the business or owner's name.

Bleep. I wish I could do math the way Sawyer could. I could do an auto-sum in the file, but I didn't want to manipulate the file in any way.

I let out a groan.

"What's wrong?" Vee asked, bringing the tea to me.

"I need our human calculator."

"Let me see." She studied the numbers for a minute, mumbling. "Yeah, these subtotals are all short."

"What?" Could everyone in the world do math in their head but me?

"Yeah, Sawyer taught me some tricks." She started talking about place values, carrying numbers, and estimates. I stared at her, really trying to understand what she was saying. If it didn't have to do with cups and teaspoons, I didn't really know it. "And that's it. Got it?"

"Let's just say I do. Where did the money go?"

"Well, that's what I assume we have to find in all of this." She started clicking through the tabs and scrolling around. "Oh, here. If we add up the different subtotals, it looks like the difference was deposited, um, let's see ... into another bank account, or maybe the same one. I can't tell."

"Whoa. Let me compare to this one." I grabbed the printed one to compare the account numbers. "Um, same number."

"Wonder who owns this?"

"No idea. Do we know anyone who works in banking?"

"I don't think so." I racked my brain, but most everyone I knew worked in a restaurant or, as in my best friends, the post office.

"Didn't your Aunt Rita date that one guy? The one that is a bank manager."

"I have no idea."

"Yeah, his name was Martin Rivera. They dated for a year or so right after we graduated high school."

"How do you remember that?"

"I don't know." She shrugged, smiling at me.

"You're weird, but I love you. I doubt that this Martin Rivera is still a bank manager, though. That was nearly twenty years ago."

"Isn't it worth asking Rita if she kept in touch with him? You never know."

I checked the time. After ten, there was no way I could ask her tonight. She and Granny were early to bed, early to rise types.

"I will call her tomorrow, and I probably need to call Mr. Jones, too. See if he knows anything about the school's budget or who oversees it."

"Good plan." She yawned. "I'm going to bed. Early day tomorrow."

"Remember when we would stay out all night and still be at work first thing in the morning?"

"Ah, the good ole days." She laughed as she took our mugs to the sink. "Night, girl."

"Night."

I sat there a bit longer, scrolling through the various documents and spreadsheets. I tried to do the math, but I ended up pulling out my phone to use the calculator on it.

Dang, if this is right, there were thousands or maybe a million deposited into this other account. My eyes were crossing, so I made some notes and then shut things down.

Tomorrow I will talk to Noah about what I found. Perhaps he knew someone who could help with identifying the owner of the bank account.

Chapter Eleven

"This is crazy," Noah said, as he looked through what we'd found. "There are hundreds of thousands transferred to this account over a couple of years. That has to add up to nearly three million dollars being embezzled."

"How has nobody noticed?"

"Not nobody. Colt noticed." He frowned.

"True." I nodded. "What do we do now?"

"I don't know yet."

"Well, what I was thinking, and wanted to get your thought on, is finding a banker to talk to and also going to talk to Mr. Jones."

"Your old teacher?"

"Yeah, most of this is coming from his department."

"Yes, and what if he is involved? You will just be painting a big ole target on your back."

"Wait. No, he can't be involved. He's a good guy."

I hadn't thought of that. Why hadn't I thought of that? Oh, I know why, because it was crazy. He was my mentor, my teacher, and my friend. There was no way he would siphon money from the school. I just couldn't believe it.

"You thought the same about Jenn and look what happened."

I half laughed at his statement. It was sad, but true. I couldn't argue with him about that.

"You are not going to let me live that down, are you?"

"Not as long as I live. I have a good instinct about these things. You like to see the good in everyone, which is not always a bad thing."

"So, you didn't have that instinct when we hired her?"

"Well, you got me there." He chuckled. "So, next steps?"

"Well, do you know anyone in banking? Someone that can look up who owns this account?"

"I'll have to think about it. And for the school, should we set up a meeting with your teacher?"

"I thought you didn't want to do that, you know, in case he is involved?" I pointed out.

"I have an idea on that." He sat forward excitedly. "We just go talk to him, get a feel for things. I test my instincts on him and see if I think he is involved. But we don't ask him about the money or the budget."

"Um, okay. What do we ask him then?"

"Weren't you thinking about starting a kind of apprentice or intern type of program?"

"Oh, yeah, I forgot about that." It was something I had talked about when we were still in the planning stage of the restaurant. "I can't believe you remembered."

"What do you think? We could go in there under the guise of looking for an apprentice. Then we can ask him questions about the students, the program, maybe how the budget works, if things seem to flow that way."

"What does the budget have to do with it?"

"I don't know, but we can just ask questions, and maybe it will seem more natural in the conversation."

"Alrighty, I will call him to set something up, but I also think we should make this happen and actually bring someone in. I think it would be awesome."

I thought back to the snickerdoodles I had at the art festival a few months ago from the Culinary Arts School booth. One of the students had made them. They were some of the best I had ever had. Even today, the craving for them was gnawing at me.

I wonder if she was still a student there. We could really use that kind of talent here.

"Great. I'll let you handle the kitchen questions, and I can ask the business ones."

"It's a plan then." I nodded and stood to go prep for the day.

Calling Duncan Jones would have to wait until this afternoon once the lunch rush had ended. At least it would give me some time to think about what we would want in an apprentice and how many we should hire. One pastry and one for the line, I think, could work.

I was thankful they had year-round school, because it was summer, and most schools would be closed. They had different breaks than the more traditional school year. Since most of the students had troubled backgrounds, this was a good schedule, as it kept them busy. Well, at least gave them less chances to get into trouble.

Hours later, the cooking was done, and Parker had come in for the evening shift. I had formulated a plan and now just needed to call Mr. Jones to ask him about it.

I washed my hands and headed into the office. Cullen and Noah were discussing the day. I smiled, grabbed my stuff, and then headed out. There wasn't much for me to do now that my team was running so well. I loved it.

I stopped by the bar for a peach lemonade to-go, then I was on my way. In the car, I connected my phone to bluetooth and pushed the button labeled Duncan Jones.

"Hello, this is Duncan Jones," His voice came over the speakers.

"Hi, Mr. Jones. This is Jessica Vasquez. How are you?"

"Oh, Jessie, it's nice to hear from you. I'm well. How are you?"

"I'm good."

"So, what can I do for you?" he asked.

"I wanted to see if I could come by and talk to you about something we are thinking about starting at the restaurant."

"Oh, that sounds interesting. What are you thinking?"

"Well, my general manager and I think it would be a nice partnership with the school to start an apprenticeship. We would want one pastry and one line cook apprentice that would work alongside of my employees and learn from them."

"That would be amazing. It would open up a lot of opportunities for the students and maybe other restaurant owners would hear and be interested as well. Yes, Jessie, yes, let's make this happen."

"Great. Can we set up a time for Noah and me to come by to discuss it with you? Maybe I can show him around a bit, and we can work out details with you."

"Definitely. Could you come by on Friday, say around 10 am?"

I was sure I could get June or Parker to work my shift so I could go during school hours. Cullen was going to be doing a full shift that day for Noah, so I thought we could do this.

"Yes, we'll be there."

After another few minutes of small talk, we hung up. I hit the button for Noah.

"Miss me already?" He laughed.

"Um, yeah, that's it." I chuckled. "But I wanted to let you know I talked to Mr. Jones. He said we could come by Friday morning around ten. Would that work for you?"

"Yeah, I was going to help April with something, but I'll ask to meet her later."

"Are you sure?"

"Yeah, it wasn't urgent."

"Great!"

"See ya tomorrow."

After we hung up, I stared forward watching the cars, wondering if I should call Aunt Rita. I didn't remember her ex-boyfriend, Martin Rivera, but Vee had a better memory of these things.

But if I asked her, it would tip her off that something was going on. How would I explain why I needed to know? If she never dated a Martin Rivera who was a bank manager, it would be even tougher to explain.

Maybe if we went to Sunday dinner, I would see if I could find time to bring it up, but over the phone wasn't the right way.

Chapter Twelve

Noah met me at the school. I arrived as he was parking. I found a spot two down from him. Once I was parked, Noah walked to my car.

"Good morning," I greeted, as I gathered my purse and climbed out of my car.

"Morning."

"You ready?"

"Yep, are you?"

"I think so. I'm oddly nervous about this. It feels deceptive."

I looked up at my alma mater. It looked oddly small and yet so very familiar with the weathered concrete exterior and dingy windows. It wasn't exactly inviting from this view, but I knew how welcoming it had been to this lost kid once upon a time.

"But it's not. You are offering two students a chance to work at one of the most popular restaurants under you, an award-winning chef."

"Okay, true, true, but the rest of it feels … icky."

"Agree to disagree," he said. "My friend was killed. I want answers."

I nodded as we reached the door. We were greeted by the school's secretary, Shirley Wolfe.

"Jessica Vasquez! I can't believe it. We have a celebrity in our building!" She squealed and came around the counter to hug me.

"Oh, it's so nice to see you, Ms. Wolfe."

"Oh, please, call me Shirley."

"Okay, thank you." I smiled. "This is my friend and general manager, Noah Linwood. We're here to meet with Mr. Jones."

"Oh, yes, yes, of course. Duncan mentioned y'all were coming in to talk to some of the students about an apprenticeship or something."

"Yes, that's right. I thought it would be a good opportunity to help and mentor some of the students."

"Well, aren't you the best. I'll just need to see your license and get you checked in." She jogged around the counter to her computer.

I took her in. The woman who had been like a favorite auntie to us students. She always had candy on her desk or a spare umbrella if you didn't have one.

She had aged well for sixty-eight. Not looking a day over fifty. Hardly a wrinkle, dark hair, and was still quite quick and nimble.

We handed over our driver's licenses. She scanned it into a little printer, which I could see populated something on her screen while simultaneously printing out a sticky name badge.

"I just can't believe you are here! It has been so long."

"I know. I have been meaning to get over here, but the restaurant has kept me quite busy this past year. From getting it set up to running it the past five months or so."

"Well, we are just so proud of you around here. I haven't made it out there to eat yet myself, but everyone raves about it, especially that alphabet soup."

"Yeah, that's a favorite. You'll need to come by."

"I will definitely make an effort to get over there."

"Yes, just let me know if you do. I'll come say hi."

"I will." She smiled, handing us each a badge and our licenses back. "Well, here you are. You know the way, I assume."

"Yes, thank you."

"My pleasure, and it was so good to see you again." She waved. "Oh, and nice to meet you, Noah."

He smiled as we walked out into the hallway. I could smell a mix of things, from motor oil to hairspray mixed with a sweet banana smell.

Oh, I hope they have banana bread or muffins.

We arrived at the school's culinary classroom. It was like stepping back in time. I immediately became that sixteen-year-old rebel who came here to avoid punishment. It changed my life and allowed me to find my passion.

The students were huddled around one of the cooking stations where Mr. Jones was demonstrating how to cut up a whole chicken.

"Then if you lift the chicken a bit, cut downward through the rib cage and into the shoulder joints, which will separate the breast from the back."

The students took notes and then waited for the next step.

"Um, hello," I said before he started cutting again. I didn't want to distract him.

"Oh, Chef Jessica and Mr. Noah Linwood are here from The Crock Pot restaurant. I believe you all remember me talking about them, and how Jess was one of my former students," Mr. Jones said.

The students nodded. Some smiled, some simply stared.

He smiled at us. "We are happy to have you both. Please pull up a stool and join us. We are just finishing up this lesson and then I'll have them break up into groups to practice."

"Fun."

Noah and I pulled up stools near the station to watch from the sidelines. Mr. Jones showed how to cut the breasts and then cut each breast into two pieces.

"And there you have it. A whole chicken cut down into ten pieces. As I mentioned, you can leave the legs and drumsticks together to make a leg quarter. Also, cutting the breasts into two pieces is optional. It just depends on what you are cooking." He smiled over at me. "Now, please break up into your teams and practice. Chef Jessica and I will be available to assist where necessary." He winked at me.

"Yes, sir." They said in unison and then divided up into three-person teams, moving to their assigned work stations to begin working.

"Remember this?" he asked, as he washed up his station, then his hands.

"I do. It was right after this that I made my first pot of caldo de pollo. My granny was so proud that I had learned her recipe and even cut up my chicken like she does."

"That's what I hope everyone of them can learn. To take these lessons and apply them to their real lives. Just like you, they come from rough family situations, food insecurities, family members on drugs or in prison. You know."

"Oh, yes, I do."

I was one of those with a family member in prison. No idea how different my life would have been had my father not killed that man. It was something I had thought about often when I was a teenager, but not as much now as an adult.

"Let's do a lap to check progress and then we can discuss business."

Noah followed us as we moved around the four stations of students. One group was arguing about the directions.

I recognized one of the students as the baker of the snickerdoodles I had enjoyed so much at the festival. So, I stopped there as Mr. Jones and Noah moved on. I wanted to observe her a bit.

She was the one doing the cutting, and the one that knew how to cut the legs off first. There were actually many ways to do it, but given the lesson, she knew to follow his direction.

"He said to cut along here," one was saying.

"No, we need to cut the legs off first." The snickerdoodle baker argued.

"Chef?" the last girl asked me.

"Well, you are both sort of right. Typically, with this method, we like to cut the legs, including the thighs, off first, and then you will cut along the ribs there." I pointed.

"Ooohhh." They got back to work.

She easily cut the leg quarters, then separated the breasts from the ribs. No hesitation, no fear. All skills. I definitely wanted her to come work for us, but I would need to see others. After a moment, I moved to the next station. Nobody caught my attention here, but the one cutting nearly lost a finger.

"Whoa, hold," I said. "Move your hand and curl that finger back. There you go."

"Thanks, Chef."

"Not a problem. Just keep an eye and focus. Nobody loses a finger, right?"

Mr. Jones used to say that to us. I think of it sometimes while I chop. It always puts a smile on my face.

"Yes, Chef," he said.

He went to cut, and the knife slipped. I got the feeling that I was making him nervous, so I moved on. After I had observed each group, I joined Noah and Mr. Jones by the teacher's station.

"What did you think?"

"That table has potential, especially the tall girl in the middle."

"Shayla. She's good."

"She's the one who made the snickerdoodles at last quarters art festival, right?"

"She is. Here, let me show you something." He gestured for us to follow him.

We walked to the cooking area. Here were piles of banana bread. I knew I had smelled banana bread.

Each had a name tag in front of them, but I couldn't quite read them all. He selected one from the counter, cut a few pieces from it, and then handed it on a napkin to both Noah and me.

I looked it over, smelling it, feeling the texture, and then took a bite.

"Oh, wow. That's heavenly. It is dense but light and moist. Just enough banana but not overpowering and you really get a nice vanilla taste. Nothing fake about it."

"That's Shayla."

"Impressive." I looked over at the students, but specifically at Shayla. The students had switched who was doing the butchering. Shayla was coaching the girl on their team. "She has some leadership skills."

"Yes, definitely. She is her section lead and mentors the less experienced or those struggling." He looked at me. "Sounds like someone else I know."

"Well, I couldn't let them struggle." I chuckled. "Noah, you had questions, right?"

My mind had gone blank on things we'd discussed. I just knew I wanted Shayla to come work with us. She would be a wonderful addition. I could see a lot of potential in her.

I shoved another piece of the banana bread in my mouth as I listened to Noah ask about the program. After random questions about the school and program in general, he got to the meat of why we were truly here, and my ears were wide open.

"So, forgive me for this next line of questions. It is just the accountant and manager in me. It must take a lot of funding to run this place."

"Oh, yeah, it does. That's why we fundraise. It helps supplement the school's budget."

"Are you in control of the budget allocation? Meaning, do you have control of the spending?"

Oh, Noah went for it. I tried to keep my face neutral, as if I wasn't really listening or interested, but if I were sitting, I would be on the edge of my seat.

"I have some input, but the way it works for our school is the school board holds the budget and manages allocation. It is primarily controlled by the superintendent, along with the city council. I put in my requests each quarter, depending on what food we need to order, etc. and then they approve it."

"Ah, makes sense. What about your fundraising money? How does that work?"

"I have all the control of that money. We use it to help fund field trips and to allow us to go to competitions."

"Perfect."

"What other questions do you have?"

"I don't have any others, but I think we are both ready to discuss details for the apprenticeship. Like, what do you need from us and who do you recommend?"

"I'm so excited about this. I love this idea." Mr. Jones glowed. I knew he wanted to expand their impact and reach within the community. "Basically, I thought that this could be an after school job situation. I don't want them missing school time. But I would give them extra credit and more responsibilities. They could come teach the others some of what they are learning."

"That sounds good to us," Noah said, then looked at me for confirmation. "Chef?"

"Yes, I think it is a win-win-win. Win for the school, win for us, and big win for the students."

"Now what do we do?"

"I already know I'd like to extend an offer to Shayla." I whispered her name, not wanting to give the students a reason to look at us. Thankfully, they were still busy with their chickens. The last member in each team was working through their chicken. "But is there another one or two that you think we should talk to?"

He studied his students for a moment.

"Yeah, I know two I think I'd recommend, but definitely Shayla. She's my top student. Nobody else comes close." He kept his voice low. "Jacoby and Brooklynne are my next two strongest, but they could use some additional guidance and I think you'd be the perfect mentor for them."

"Okay. I trust your judgment. When can I talk to them?"

"Right now. It looks like they are done." Mr. Jones walked back to the students and started inspecting their work. "Great. This looks impressive. Shayla, could you show Mr. Linwood and Chef Jessica to my office?"

"Yes, sir." She gestured for us to follow her, then she gestured into his office. "Here you are."

"Thanks. Actually, we wanted to talk to you. Join us?" I said, motioning for her to sit as we took seats ourselves. She eyed me as she sat. "It's good, I promise."

"Okay, Chef."

"We have been talking to Mr. Jones about an opportunity to hire students from here as apprentices. It would mean learning and working with me and my team."

I paused to give her a chance to respond or ask questions. She simply nodded, but her face remained stoic. What is her story? I hadn't seen her smile yet. Poor girl.

Perhaps she had been let down one too many times. Maybe she had to grow up too fast. Whatever it was, I hoped to change her life like mine was.

"Anyway, I wanted to offer you one of the two spots. You would work mostly with Natalie, who is my current pastry chef, but you would have chances to work at the other stations, too. Oh, and you would get paid by me and extra credit here at school."

"Really? You want me to work for you?" Tears formed in her eyes, causing my eyes to well up, too.

"Yes. Are you interested?"

"Yes, yes, very much." She finally smiled.

"Great! Can you start with us after school on Monday or Tuesday?"

We would need to do some paperwork so not sure how quickly we'd get that done.

"Really?" she squealed, shooting up from the chair. "Yes!"

Mr. Jones came in with two other students. He smiled.

"I guess the conversation in here went well."

"It did." I nodded.

"Mr. Jones, thank you so much for making this happen." She had tears streaming down her face. "This is going to open so many doors for me. I can finally ... well, just break the cycle."

Her face turned red. She turned her back as she grabbed a tissue from the box on his desk. I wanted to hug her, but it felt inappropriate.

The other two students looked confused. Mr. Jones simply smiled at them. Now I felt some guilt that I couldn't hire both of them. I looked at Noah. He nodded.

"We'd like to extend the same offer to both of you," I said.

"What?"

"Really?"

"Both?" Mr. Jones seemed surprised.

"Yeah, we can take all three of them," I said. Noah nodded.

I just felt like it was the right thing to do. I knew how much the opportunities I'd been given meant to me. If I could open doors for them, I was going to.

"Oh, Chef, this is amazing. Thank you."

"So, if you could all be at The Crock Pot on Monday or Tuesday, after school, we'll get you all started."

We ironed out a few more details, then Noah and I thanked them all. Shayla ran to the banana bread, grabbed one of hers, wrapped it and then handed it to me.

"I saw that you really enjoyed it. I thought we could spare one." She smiled. "Consider it a thank you."

"Oh, wow. Thank you. It was really good." I smiled. "We'll be in touch."

We waved and walked out of the room.

"Well, that went well, and you got a gift."

"Jealous?"

"Yeah, little bit." He chuckled. "But you deserve it. I'm glad you asked all three of them."

"Me too. When I saw Shayla's reaction, I knew I had to do the same for the other two. Now I just need to figure out how to keep them all busy."

"Shayla with Natalie, then split time for the other two between the sous chef and the line cooks."

"Yeah, but I do want Shayla to work the other stations, too." I paused. "But I don't have to solve it now. I have all weekend to figure it out."

"Plus, we got the answers about who else might be involved in the embezzling."

"Yes, we do," I turned towards my car. "Well, see you tomorrow?"

"Yes, after work for clue gathering."

We arrived at the office to check out.

"Did you have fun seeing the old classroom?" Shirley asked.

"Yes, it was great to remember."

"Well, don't stay gone so long the next time. Come see us sooner."

"I will and you come by the restaurant."

"Oh, I will be." She tapped a few things on the computer. "So what was the business you had with Duncan? I think you mentioned but I can't remember. Old age."

"We discussed having some of the students come to work for us. Kind of an apprenticeship."

"Well, isn't that wonderful." She smiled. "Alright, y'all are checked out. I guess I'll see you around."

"Thank you. It was good to see you."

"Good to see you."

Out in the parking lot, Noah slowly turned to face me. His expression was peculiar, almost as if he'd smelled something bad.

"There was something off about her body language."

"What? You aren't suggesting she's a suspect, are you?"

"Why did she have you repeat why we were here? Why did she narrow her eyes when you answered?"

I stared at him. Shirley Wolfe was just a sweet older lady. She was everyone's mom or favorite aunt.

"I didn't notice that. Did she?"

"Yes, she did. Plus, she even mentioned that Duncan had already told her why we were here and then asked us again. Why?"

He might have a point, but I didn't want to think about that. He was reading too much into it.

"You are crazy."

"I know it sounds crazy and out of left field, but just think about it."

"Okay, fine. I will think about." I doubted I would change my mind, but I would at least think about it. "See you tomorrow."

"Yep, work and then we'll do that board."

"I can't wait. Vee is so crazy excited."

"She watches too many crime shows." Noah laughed as he opened his car door.

I laughed, waving as I climbed into my car.

Mr. Jones had confirmed that the superintendent was primarily responsible for the budget allocation. That meant one thing, we would have to look at Superintendent Van Rhodes. Just because he had control, doesn't mean he was the one, but that's what we needed to figure out.

I guess tomorrow, we would add him to the clue board. However, I couldn't, in any scenario, find a reason to add Shirley, and I thought about it.

Chapter Thirteen

Today we were putting together the investigation board or clues board. Roy Hart, Sawyer's dad, was over building it while I was working. The plan was for Noah to follow me home so we could all put the clues together and start brainstorming.

We'd order pizza and work until we either solved it or until we were cross-eyed and tired.

I just had to get through my shift. For some reason, even though we weren't exactly slow, today was dragging. At one point, Noah came to talk to me.

"Hey."

"Hey." I continued to work on the dish in front of me.

"I'm bored." He drummed his fingers on my station and sighed.

"It feels like the clock isn't moving, right?"

"Yeah, I think because we're going to have that fun craft tonight." He chuckled, scanning to make sure nobody was paying attention to us. They weren't.

"I don't know if we have enough to add to it yet, but it will be a start."

"Yeah, but we can add as we go."

"True, true."

"Now, if the clock would just speed up!" He grumbled and then left me to finish cooking.

I thought about the clues we had, like the grainy pictures of Chief Stone and Finance Director Davis Campbell together. We had embezzled money from the school to some random bank account. We knew now that the superintendent oversaw allocation of the school budget with the support of the city council. So that could be the superintendent alone or a member of the city council.

I thought about what Noah said about Shirley Wolfe. I couldn't for the life of me think of how she would be involved. She was the sweet lady who greeted visitors, answered the phones, and let us sit inside the office when our ride home was running late. She smelled like baby powder and peppermint.

No, it was either the Superintendent Van Rhodes or someone on the city council or both.

A couple hours later, Parker arrived. He was the chef for the night.

"How was it today?"

"Not bad. A little slow, or maybe I'm just used to the pace now."

"Well, that's either good or bad, I guess."

"Yep." I chuckled. "Soup of the day is potato leek."

"Sounds good. Night, Chef."

"Night."

I went to the office to grab my stuff. Noah was just walking out.

"You ready?" he asked.

"Yep."

"Night, y'all," Cullen yelled as we left.

We waved and walked to the parking lot.

"You have the USB?"

"I do." He tapped his pocket.

"Well, then follow me."

We pulled down my street roughly ten minutes later. I parked in my usual spot and pointed Noah to the one behind me.

"No reserved spots?" he asked, climbing out of his car, grabbing a laptop bag from his back seat.

"Nay, and nobody usually parks in that one, anyway."

"Nice place." He glanced around.

"Thanks. Yeah, we've been here a few years now."

"It's a quiet block?"

"Yep, mostly retired folks or roommate situations like us."

"Nice."

"Well, come on in." I pushed open the door. "Hey, y'all. I brought home company!"

Vee came running. "Riley is here," she whispered. "Hi, Noah."

"Hi." He smiled.

"Oh, boy." I looked around. "Is Roy still here?"

"Yeah, they are all out back at the moment, but he did an amazing job on the board. Come see."

"Who is Riley?" he whispered to me.

"Sawyer's annoying new girlfriend," I whispered back. "But we love him so trying to be supportive."

"Ah, I understand."

We went into the extra room downstairs. We didn't use it, but it was intended as an office or flex space.

"Oh wow, you said big, but I didn't know you meant nearly the entire wall," I said, walking in. The board was wall to wall, which was fourteen feet across. Then it was four feet tall. "What will we use this for when this is done?"

"I don't know. Pictures? We've been friends for years, so we have tons together."

"That could work."

"I'll go order pizza now that y'all are here." She skipped off.

"Do you want to change?" he asked. He was dressed in slacks and a polo with our logo on it, but I was in my sweaty and dirty chef's clothes.

"If you don't mind, I'll be quick."

"No problem. I'll fire up my laptop and figure out what we want to put on the board."

"Great. I'll stick my head outside to let Sawyer know we're here."

"Perfect."

I left him there, walking to the back door. We had a small, private courtyard behind our townhouse with a grill and patio furniture. Vee had a few pots with flowers and a couple of tomato plants. There was one oak tree in the center that provided us with shade.

I took a deep breath before going outside.

"Hey, y'all. I'm home," I said, stepping out.

"Oh, Jessie!" Roy came over to hug me. "I haven't seen you in a while. You look good."

I took in the elder Hart. I hadn't seen him in several months, but he and Sawyer looked so much alike. It would be tough to imagine my friend at nearly sixty.

Roy was the same height, and his hair was long and dark, just like Sawyer's. No sign of gray hair at all. His face was a little thinner and starting to show age a bit, but otherwise, they could almost pass as twins or at least brothers.

"Thanks. You look good as well. How's work?"

"You know, I drive a truck and see the country. Not too bad."

"That's nice." I smiled at him and then looked over at Riley, who appeared to be giving me a strange look. "Hi, Riley."

"Hi, Jess."

"I saw the board, Roy. You did an awesome job."

"Aw, thanks. It was fairly simple once Vee told me her vision."

"Ha, yeah, she had a vision alright." I chuckled. "Well, I'm going to change. Noah is in the office getting started."

"Great. I'll go help him!" Sawyer jumped up and darted into the house.

Roy followed him, which left Riley and me there. Now I felt weird leaving her alone. Would she be comfortable alone?

She looked me up and down but didn't say anything. Her phone chimed.

"Excuse me." She smiled tightly, turning her back to me.

"No problem. I'm going to change, anyway."

Saved by the bell, I thought. I stepped inside, looking over my shoulder. She was whispering and eyeing me with a grimace on her face.

What the bleep?

After I freshened up and changed, I rejoined the group in the office. Vee and Riley had joined, but Vee gave me a help me look, so I went to sit on her other side.

The pizza had arrived, and they had brought in a card table, plates, and napkins. We all ate while we discussed how best to do this. None of us had done anything like this, but we had some ideas.

"This always seems to work in the movies." Vee grinned.

"I'm willing to try anything," I said.

"Me too," Noah said, biting another piece of pizza.

"Why did you order pizza? You could have brought something from the restaurant," Riley said as she picked at her slice.

All eyes turned to her then looked at me.

"Um, I guess I could have but I was working and didn't think about it. Plus, I love to support other local restaurants. This isn't from a chain."

"But isn't your job to cook? So? If you made us food, you would still be working."

"Riley," Sawyer said, calmly.

"What? I'm just saying, she is surrounded by food, and we are eating pizza."

"It's Polly's Pizza, not just any pizza," Vee added.

"I love Polly's," Noah added with a smile.

"Me too," Roy said, taking another slice.

"Sorry, fine. It was just me that thought that." Riley pouted.

Strike one for the night, Riley. I thought as I finished my slice.

After they were done eating, the guys sorted out pictures and printed pages, arranging them into some type of order that only they seemed to understand. Vee, Riley, and I sat on the sidelines watching.

"Okay, we have these two as prime suspects right now," Noah said, pinning the picture with Chief Stone and Finance Director Davis Campbell at the top. "Then we have Colt, our victim."

He took a picture of Colt and put it near the bottom. Then next to him, Noah pinned the name Imogen Potter. We could only assume that whoever killed Colt had also killed sweet Ms. Imogen Potter.

Though the police were tight-lipped on that bit of information. Media reports hadn't been much help either. Only that she had been killed in her apartment and it was under investigation. It was much the same as what was being reported about Colt, except he was shot in the street.

"Now, we need to get from here to there," he said, stepping back.

"Alright, so we need to put the spreadsheets up there, right?" I asked.

"Well, probably not all of them, so I made these." Noah held up a few pages with just words on them. One read school budget, one with the mysterious bank account on it, then the last one with J.W. Dashwood Fine Arts High School on it.

"Whoa, the school you went to?" Roy asked, pointing at me.

"Yeah."

"Mr. Jones always seemed so straight laced," Roy said, absently.

Riley didn't say much, but she seemed to be taking it all in. I was a bit uncomfortable talking about this in front of her, especially after her criticism about the food. What did we know about her? Not much other than she speaks her mind, and not in the good way.

"Oh, I should add one with his name and also the secretary's name." Noah typed on his computer, then hit print. Sawyer had brought his printer downstairs.

He and Sawyer pinned all the pages to the board. He put Mr. Jones and Shirley Wolfe next to the picture of Chief Stone and Davis Campbell. Under them, they put the things, school budget, account, and school.

They stepped back, and we all stared at it. Nobody said anything for several minutes.

"So, who are these people?" Riley asked.

We all turned to look at her. Sawyer was the only one who didn't look annoyed. He moved closer to the board.

"This is Chief Stone," He pointed to him. "Then this is the Finance Director for the city, Davis Campbell. Next, we have Van Rhodes. He is the superintendent for the schools. Then we have Mr. Jones, the teacher at the culinary arts school, and this one is Mrs. Wolfe. She's the secretary at the school."

"And you think they are all involved?" she asked.

"We don't know who is involved. That's why we're trying to figure it out," Sawyer said.

Sawyer is so patient. I couldn't say the same about myself. Why was she asking so many questions? This has nothing to do with her.

I tried to give her the benefit of the doubt though, since Sawyer had invited her. She was just trying to just fit in.

Okay, Jess, be patient.

"Well, it is obvious to me that this Mr. Jones did it," Riley said.

All of us whipped around to look at her.

"Why do you say that?" I asked. All my patience was waiting to decide if we were mad or not.

"Because he is a teacher."

"And?"

"And," she mimicked my tone. "You always hear how teachers are underpaid, and then it's possible he doesn't like how the superintendent is allocating the money. That's two reasons for it to be him. Why would these others do it? It doesn't make sense."

Noah raised an eyebrow at me. I shrugged. I couldn't believe it, but I also couldn't argue with her. Money made people do strange things, even the good ones.

I looked from the board to Noah to Vee to Riley and then back to the board again. I wanted it to be anyone else.

Sawyer walked over and put his arms around her, but over her head, he mouthed he was sorry. Maybe he realized that I didn't like her. Not that she had done anything really wrong. She was just annoying but now to suggest my former teacher as a suspect had me looking at her in an even more negative light. That one didn't sit well with me.

Vee was quiet with her arms crossed hard across her chest, which meant she was stewing. She was obviously having similar thoughts.

"We need to figure out who owns this account," Noah said.

"Yeah, any ideas on a contact at a bank?" I asked.

"You wouldn't believe me if I told you."

"Who?"

"Colt and April's dad, Ralph Evans," Noah said.

"No way. Really?"

"Yeah."

"Why didn't this Colt guy ask his dad about all this, then? I mean, why ask the two of you? Clearly, you don't know anything," Riley piped up.

Vee flew out of her chair and out of the room. Sawyer mumbled something to Riley and then followed Vee out of the room. Riley stared at me as if I did something wrong, but her bluntness was wrong in this moment.

Vee was upset on my behalf. She knew how much Duncan Jones and that school meant to me. She left to avoid causing a fight because she loved and respected Sawyer, too.

To date, no person has caused issues like this between us. I mean, I had dated a few not-so-great guys, but nobody who had caused any kind of upset like this.

Noah and Roy turned towards the board. I fidgeted with a seam on my shirt. Anything to avoid conversation with Riley.

Riley sat there with a smug look on her face. "You know I'm right," she finally said.

I looked over at Noah but didn't say a word.

After roughly ten minutes, Vee and Sawyer returned. Vee's face and eyes were red. She was not happy. I took her hand as she sat back down. Sawyer asked Riley to step out with him.

His voice carried from the other room, and though we couldn't hear his words, I knew he was angry.

"Um, so this is … uh … fun. Better than being alone in my truck." Roy chuckled.

"Yeah, entertaining." Noah laughed.

The front door slammed, then Sawyer came back in.

"So, that's over," Sawyer announced, coming back in. "I'm so sorry about that, y'all."

"You can't control other people," I said.

"Just how you react to them," Vee added. "But I am sorry about her. I know you liked her."

"It's okay. It had about run its course anyway, and I shouldn't have invited her tonight."

Even though he had said that I could tell by his deep frown that he was not so casual about her. He had a tough time finding a girl that loved playing those video games with him. Whether she was faking it or not, I knew enough about the games to know she was good at them.

I wanted to feel bad, but honestly, I didn't.

"Well, y'all have been fun, but I want to spend some time with my wife before I need to get back on the road." Roy stood. "Good to see y'all and good luck with the case. Son, love you."

"Love you, dad. Safe travels."

Sawyer hugged him, then walked him out.

Noah stood, looking at the board. "I guess I will go, too, but I'll see if I can talk to Ralph and see if he can help us."

"I'll walk you out," I said.

"Me too!" Vee popped up.

We stood outside watching Noah get in his car and drive away.

"Well, that was fun," Vee said.

"I guess."

"Since Noah is going to talk to Colt's dad, Ralph, I guess we won't need to talk to your Aunt Rita?"

"I guess not. I still don't remember this guy you mentioned, but I believe your memory over mine."

"Ha, I don't know about that, but I just remember she really seemed to like him." She turned to go back inside. "I'm going to look at the board some more."

"Me too."

As I turned to follow her, movement nearby caught my attention, but then I didn't see anything. I stared at the spot trying to see if I saw anything, but nothing.

"You coming?" she asked.

"Yeah, right behind you."

We stared at the board, talking about this person or that clue, but without more information we couldn't put this together. After another hour, we called it a night. We hadn't solved anything, but a clue board that I could take a look at any time might help me figure this out.

Chapter Fourteen

Last night had been both fun and rough. Fun to hang out and create the giant clue board, but I felt so bad for Sawyer with what happened with Riley.

Today was a new day and I had the whole day off. This afternoon, we were going to Sunday dinner at Granny Ines and Aunt Rita's house. I just hoped my awful uncle, aunt, and cousins weren't there. I wasn't in the mood for their snarky comments.

Uncle Sullivan "Sully" was my dad's older brother. He was married to Gina for thirty-five years. They had two children, Nova and Sullivan Junior, but everyone called him Junior.

We hadn't seen each other in a few months. Not since my Uncle Sully went off on my grandmother, aunt, and even brought me into it. It had been quite a memorable evening. Since then, we have avoided any time they would be at Granny's house.

But they were out of town for a vacation or something, so it was the perfect time to go.

Since I had the day off, Vee and I were going hiking together, while Sawyer stayed behind to sleep and lick his wounds.

I threw on a pair of black leggings and one of Colt's Neal Barney shirts. It was large on me, which I liked. Grabbing my shoes, I jogged down the stairs to meet Vee, but of course, I was first.

I filled our water bottles while I waited. It had been a while since I'd been able to go hiking and I couldn't wait.

Finally, I heard her bouncing down the stairs.

"I'm so excited to have you going with me today." Vee giggled.

"Me too." I shoved a few granola bars into my bag. "Your car or mine?"

"I never get to drive, so can we take mine?"

"Sounds good."

We headed out towards the state park. It would be hot and humid out today since it's August, but thankfully the trails were shady with large oaks and dense pines. They stretched their branches together and across the paths to form these wonderful canopies.

"I haven't been out here in so long," I said as we started down one of the paths. This one should take us around the lake. It was roughly three miles.

"This is my favorite place." Vee smiled, stretching her legs to keep up with me.

"Do you want me to slow my pace?"

"No, I'm used to keeping up with Sawyer and you aren't quite as fast as him."

"Should I be insulted by that?" I laughed.

"Ha, no, not at all."

We walked for a while in silence. I watched the birds flitting through the trees, squirrels running across the path in front of us before scurrying up trees on the opposite side. It was therapeutic to be out here.

It gave me time to reflect on everything going on. First, we had Colt's murder. Never having met him in person, it was weird getting to know him through this investigation. We had so much in common.

It had me wondering about all the other people I had yet to meet in the world. Someone out there could be a perfect match for me, but I may never know them.

"So, what do you think about what happened with Riley?" Vee said, breaking the silence.

"That was ... a mess. I don't know what it is about her that rubs me wrong."

"I know what it is for me. She can't keep her mouth shut."

"Well, I've never seen you get so mad before."

"Yeah, well, I just knew she was accusing your teacher and mentor. He is a good guy. I hate that he is even listed as a suspect, but for her to poke at it and then tell us we can't do this, I just couldn't sit there any more listening to her."

"Yeah, I was just in shock. I hate this for Sawyer though. He really seemed to like her."

"I know. He is usually so picky."

We reached the mid-point of the trail, pausing to look at the lake. It was beautiful. Large water birds like herons, egrets, and various ducks dotted the shore and swam through the water. It was mesmerizing to watch them, especially the ducks as they swam around. A large heron took flight and soared from one side to the other, landing lightly in the water.

Vee slipped an arm around my waist as we watched. We stood there one arm around each other, enjoying nature. After several minutes, we moved on.

We got to the far side of the lake before we saw another person. It was a lady with a border collie. He greeted us with a wag of his tail. We greeted him with pats on his head and a hello to her.

Reaching the end of the path, I took a deep cleansing breath.

"That was nice. I need to try to do this more when I'm off." I took a gulp of water.

"It was nice to do this with you again. It has been too long."

We stretched a little before climbing into her car.

"Are you going to talk to Aunt Rita about her ex-boyfriend?"

"I honestly don't know. If Ralph Evans can get the bank information, then I won't need her guy," I said.

I couldn't believe how casually Noah had mentioned that Colt's father, Ralph, was in banking and could get us the information we needed. Why hadn't he thought of that before last night?

"True, but what if he can't get it?"

"Then I guess I'll need to ask her, but I don't want to explain to her why I need it or what I'm doing. I really don't want them involved at all."

"Yeah, that makes sense."

"But I'll keep it in my back pocket, just in case."

We got parked and I saw Sawyer talking to someone at the door.

"Is that Shirley Wolfe?" Vee asked.

"Yeah, it looks like her. That's weird." I got out of the car. "Hi, Shirley."

"Oh, Jessie, there you are. Hi." She came towards me, hugging me. "I found a few pictures from your first competition, and I thought you might like to have them. After you came by the other day, I ran across them, so I looked up your address and here I am."

She thrust a large envelope my way.

"Oh, thanks." I didn't mention that I had all the pictures. They were displayed near the door of my restaurant. "This is sweet."

I wanted to add the words "but weird" to the end of that statement, but I bit my tongue.

"Well, that was all. I just wanted to say hi and give you those. Mission accomplished." She laughed, waving as she walked down the sidewalk and around the block. Before she turned at the corner, she looked our way. Catching us looking, she waved as she disappeared.

"Is it weird that she didn't go to a car?" Vee pointed out.

"Yeah, that whole thing was strange." I looked at Sawyer. "What did she say before we got here?"

"Not much. She'd just gotten here."

"Uh, well, okay."

We went inside. Sawyer asked about the hike and then we got ready to head over for dinner. I threw the envelope on my dresser as I peeled off my clothes to shower. I didn't give it another thought.

Two hours later, we were sitting around the table and Granny Ines was piling food on the table while Aunt Rita served us drinks.

"We are so happy you three are here." Rita swayed and swooned around the table. She was always dancing in her head.

"Thank you for having us." Sawyer grinned. He had been a quieter version of himself.

It made me a bit sad that I had any hand in his breakup, but even after talking it out with Vee, I did nothing wrong. He had invited her and then she popped off with her crazy opinion.

Calm down, Jess, it's over, I told myself.

Granny said a prayer over the food before we ate. She'd made tacos with her homemade tortillas, pico de gallo, and rice and beans. There were also chicken flautas and stuffed peppers. This is what I'd grown up eating and loving. It sent me right back to childhood.

"So, tell me how is the restaurant going?" Granny asked.

"It's going well. We have the new assistant manager in place. He's quiet, but fits in."

"And you added the students from your school?" It was part statement, part question.

"Yes, did I tell you that already?"

"No, I ran into Shirley Wolfe recently. She told me."

Wow, I hadn't seen her in years but now she seemed to be popping up everywhere.

"Ah. Yeah, they are working out well. I will likely be offering them full-time positions when they graduate."

"That's so wonderful that you can do that. I know how much Duncan meant to you. To give back to the school, well, it has come full circle," Aunt Rita said.

"Rita," Vee said. "I saw someone at the post office that reminded me of that guy you used to date. I think his name was Martin something and he worked at a bank."

Aunt Rita froze, her fork an inch from her mouth. A blush formed from her face down her neck to her chest.

"Oh, yeah," she stammered. "I did. Wow, you have a good memory."

"Was it him?" Granny asked.

"No, name was Phil Rodriguez, but it reminded me of that guy and you." Vee smiled with such innocence that if I hadn't known why she was asking, I would have assumed it was that simple.

"Uh, I haven't thought of him in years."

"He was Rita's one who got away," Granny said, flatly.

"Mother!"

"Well, it's true. And if I hadn't been so sick that year, you might have gotten married. He just wasn't prepared for a mother-in-law."

"What happened to him?" Vee probed.

Sawyer and I shared a look that I hope nobody else caught.

"He ended up meeting someone and they moved to Florida."

That answers that question. Even if it wasn't my plan to ask, since I was hoping for Colt's dad, Ralph, to answer that question, it was still good to know that our back-up plan was a no-go.

"Aw, I'm sorry that I brought it up." Vee touched Aunt Rita's hand.

"Thanks."

We wrapped up our dinner with my grandmother's cinnamon cookies. They were different than snickerdoodles but perfect for a nice after dinner treat.

"Sorry, I know you weren't going to ask about her boyfriend, but I thought we might as well know if she was still in touch with him," Vee said, once we were back in the car.

"I figured. It's good to know."

"I instantly regretted asking when I saw her face though."

"I feel awful for being so wrapped up in myself back then. I didn't even realize how hurt she was by him."

"And what is with Shirley Wolfe being everywhere these days?" Sawyer asked.

"I know. I literally was thinking the same thing earlier."

"I guess it's when you don't see someone for a while, and then you start seeing them everywhere."

"Like Carlos."

"Like Chuck." I gagged.

"Like Emma."

"Or my mother."

"Oh, I saw Samuel the other day. He stopped by the post office to send a package."

"Weird."

We pulled up to the house. The hair on the back of my neck stood. I looked around like a crazy person before getting out.

"What's wrong?" Sawyer said, sticking his head back inside.

"I don't know. I just feel like … someone is watching." I looked around again.

They both started looking around too.

"I don't see anything," she whispered.

"I'm probably just being paranoid with everything going on." I slid out of the car but hustled up the steps to our front door and waited with my back to the wall for Sawyer to unlock it for us.

Movement across the street caused us all to freeze and look. A large black and white cat strolled down the street.

"A cat." Vee exhaled.

"I'll just be glad when this is over," I said as we all made it safely inside our house.

Chapter Fifteen

Monday, Noah came over to my station after the lunch rush.

"Ralph Evans is here. Do you have time to come to the office?"

"Hm, yeah, I think so. Let me just finish this dish." I flipped the fish. "Hannah, will you be able to take over for me after this?"

"Yes, Chef."

I took the salmon out, plating it and then adding the scalloped potatoes and spinach to the plate.

"Order up!" I hit the bell, then nodded to Hannah, who came to take over my station.

I washed my hands and smoothed my hair before heading to the office. My reflection showed a hot, sweaty mess of a person.

Icky. I splashed cool water on my face, then dried it. *Better.*

"Ralph, this is Jessica Vasquez," Noah said, when I walked into the office.

I took him in. He looked a lot like Colt, or should I say, Colt looked like him. They had the same kind eyes and smile. His hair was now a strawberry gray color. It must have once been the same red as April and Colt's.

"Hi, nice to meet you," we said at the same time.

"Thank you for coming," I added.

"If it helps find who killed my son, I am happy to help," he said, then his face fell, taking on a stern expression. "Though I don't think either of you should be involved in this."

His tone caused a chill to run down my spine, which was crazy because he didn't make a threat. I think it was just the mere thought of Colt being gunned down in the street over this. His dad was a reminder of that, but his extreme frown as he stared at me didn't help.

Noah didn't seem bothered by the comment, but I wanted to ask more. Unfortunately, before I could figure out what I wanted to ask, Noah got down to business.

"Well, here is the account number." Noah handed them to him.

Ralph pulled out a laptop and connected it to our Wi-Fi. We watched as he clicked and typed and clicked some more. He hemmed and hummed as he moved around.

I don't know what he was doing, as the screen kept changing too quickly. I simply watched and waited, hoping he had the answer we needed.

"Okay, so it looks like this is just a shell account. Everything points to another account, but I can't tell who owns it." He clicked a few things. "It's another company, but usually you can see who owns it."

He typed and clicked around, grunting a few frustrated curse words, then tried a few other things.

"Yeah, nothing," he mumbled.

"But, you're saying it goes from one account to another and that is owned by some mysterious company?" Noah asked.

"Yep. See."

Together, they flipped back through all the screens. Noah seemed to know what he was looking at. I tried to follow, but they were going too quickly, and I didn't understand the accounting and banking jargon.

I knew some just from owning the business and learning from Noah, but they had gone deeper than my knowledge.

"Whoa, now we need to figure out this company." Noah hopped on our computer and tried doing some searches. "There is a board of directors, but I don't recognize any of these names. They are all out of state as is the address."

"This doesn't make sense," Ralph said.

"Well, at least you got us one of the answers we needed. I knew this wasn't going to be easy. Colt had been working on this for a while, or so it seems," Noah offered.

"I was hoping we would find more. This has been a bad dream that I wish I could wake from," Ralph said.

"Yeah, me too," Noah said with a frown.

"Colt was a smart kid. I can't believe he got himself wrapped up in such a mess."

"I know," Noah said.

"Welp, I better get going. The wife isn't doing well these days and I hate leaving her for long." He closed his laptop as he stood. "It was nice to meet you, Jessica."

"Nice to meet you, too and thank you for the help."

He stared at me for a moment, causing me to fidget under the intense look. It was only a split second, but it felt like much longer.

"Like I said, anything to help find who did this. My son was a good guy but had gotten himself into some bad stuff." He paused. "It would be best if you stay out of it. You don't know who you are messing with."

I startled at his comment, then looked at Noah. He seemed unfazed, so I shook it off as a friendly warning. Maybe he just didn't want us to follow the same fate as his son.

I plastered on a smile.

"I'll walk you out."

"No need. I know the way and I'm sure you all have to get back to work. I just wanted to help."

He walked out. I turned to Noah, who was tapping away on the computer.

"That was weird, right?"

"Which part?"

"I don't know. I just ... had a weird vibe." I was still stuck on his almost threatening tone and his awkward staring. I tried to brush it off as grief over his son.

"Oh, now you're having weird vibes about people," he turned, chuckling. "But yeah, Ralph is a weirdo."

I stewed on the interaction with Ralph for the rest of my shift. It felt like he had warned us against looking into things. Not once, but twice. Was it because he wanted to keep us safe or because he was involved?

"Chef, there is a girl here to see you," Marco said.

I checked the time. Nearly the end of my shift. Who was this?

"I'll be right there." I turned to Hannah. "Should be slow, but can you manage things until I get back or June arrives?"

"Of course."

"Great. Marco, tell her I'll be right there. Offer her a drink and a seat at the bar."

"Yes, Chef." He turned out of the kitchen.

I went to wash up and then walked out to the dining room. Looking over at the bar, I saw Riley.

What the bleep? I thought as I walked towards her.

"Um, hi, Riley. Can I help you?"

"Yeah, you can. You can tell me what the heck you did to Sawyer for him to end it with me?"

"Why would I know? That was between the two of you."

"He said I was rude to you. When? What did you say to him?"

"I didn't say anything. I didn't have to. You were rude the other night about my teacher and to me."

"It might have been rude, but I'm not wrong. You don't know what you have gotten yourself into or the people you are messing with! You should just stop!"

She flipped her hair, storming out without a backward glance.

I stared at her, mouth open. Immediately my brain asked if she was involved?

Holy moly!

I looked around to see if anyone else had heard, but my employees were working away. They were cleaning and setting up for dinner. To be fair, even if her words were sharp, her voice never rose above a whisper.

I hurried to the office.

"Noah, holy, Noah."

"What?"

"Riley was just here."

"Sawyer's Riley?"

"Yeah, that one. She threatened or warned me. I guess not everything is a threat, but she said I didn't know who I was messing with, and I should stop. How would you take that?"

He jumped up. "Like a threat. What did you say to that?"

"She stormed out before I could process what she'd just said."

"You'll need to add her to the suspect list when you get home."

"Yeah, you're right."

It would hurt Sawyer's feelings, but with her warning, I had to. I might add Ralph as well. Something felt off about his words or his tone. Noah wouldn't like that, but I didn't like that Shirley and Mr. Jones had been listed as suspects. None of this felt good.

After work, I decided to head over to city hall. I'm not sure why or what I hoped to find, but I figured it couldn't hurt to just look around. It just seemed like the next logical place to look for clues.

I found a parking spot fairly easily. The lot seemed only about half as full as I've seen it in the past. I supposed it was nearing the end of the workday for everyone.

Walking across the park-like front of city hall, I took in the care and love that the town put into landscaping. It wasn't just city hall; it was the entire town, but here there was the lush green grass, neatly trimmed scrubs, and brightly colored flowers that lined the sidewalk.

There was also a rose garden to the right side that was dedicated to the nurses at the hospital. The garden was laid out in a maze with a fountain at the center and benches placed in the best viewing spots. It was in full bloom at the moment, and I loved all the bright flowers. It was tempting to sidetrack and take a stroll through it.

But no, I continued and soon I was stepping into the marble and brass front foyer and was greeted by the blast of air conditioning. It felt good after being in the hot kitchen and then the warm outdoors. The heat was another good reason to skip the rose garden.

I looked left and right, trying to decide what to do here. I saw an electronic bulletin board ahead of me, which gave me an idea. The sign was cycling through the various announcements, so I had to wait for the one I was looking for.

Ah, here it is. City Council meeting on Wednesday at 7 p.m. Okay, I could do that.

I turned to leave and nearly ran into someone.

"Oh, I'm sorry about that." I blushed.

"That's okay. Oh, hey, you're Chef Jessica, right?"

"Yes." I looked at him and then realized it was Superintendent Van Rhodes.

"I'm Van, the superintendent of the schools. We are very proud of your success as one of the best, most successful students to come out of our culinary arts program." He beamed with pride as if he had something to do with it.

"Well, thank you."

"What are you doing here?" He looked over me to the sign behind me as if it would tell him.

"Oh, yeah, I was just thinking of coming to the city council meeting and I was checking the time."

"You could have checked online."

"Duh, yeah, I should have thought of that."

"Do you have business with the council?"

"No, no. Just thinking that as a new business owner, I would like to get more involved in city business. You know, understand the projects, how money is spent, and what I can do to help."

He eyed me, a deep frown on his face. Thanks to Noah, I was starting to pay more attention to the things people didn't say.

"That sounds very responsible of you. I wish more business owners and citizens would take an interest in it. Well, I'll see you there. Gotta get to a meeting." He tapped the planner he was carrying.

"I will see you then." I hurriedly walked out, not looking back.

Once in my car, I finally let out my breath. That was tense. Could he tell I was nervous? I was definitely going to add an extra exclamation point to his name when I got home. Plus, I would add Riley and Ralph, too.

Chapter Sixteen

Our new apprentices started yesterday. We had originally agreed on them starting Monday, but we had to push it one day because of their schedules, but also, we had to get our paperwork in order.

They were all on time and eager to get started. They asked a ton of questions. My staff welcomed them with open arms and Natalie, especially, was eager to have an apprentice working with her.

The restaurant had been so busy, she barely had time to breathe most days. I felt bad, and I'd jump in when I could to help, but I was never a great baker. My line cooks took turns here and there, but what she needed was a true pastry chef, even if that chef was still in school.

Yesterday, I got them all started and then June took over the evening shift, so I was anxious to hear how their first day went.

Shayla was the first to arrive.

"Hi, Chef."

"Hi, Shayla. Good to see you again."

"Thanks." She looked around, then down at her feet.

"You okay?"

"Yeah, yeah, just nervous. Yesterday was … eye-opening."

"Busy?"

"Very, but I loved each moment. I am just hoping I didn't slow Chef Natalie down too much."

"Well, the feedback I got was glowing, so just do whatever you did yesterday, and you should be fine."

"Really? Thanks, Chef." Her entire face brightened. She skipped to the pastry station and was greeted by an enthusiastic Natalie. They immediately got to work.

Next Jacoby arrived. I was going to have him work with my evening line cook, Stelly. He had worked with June last night, and I wanted to switch it up. That meant Brooklynne would be working with June, but I would get her started for the day.

"Afternoon, Brooklynne. You're with me today and then you'll work with Chef June tonight."

"That's awesome, Chef."

I started showing her how we prep between shifts, and then a ticket printed. Stelly had Jacoby call out the order.

"Cucumber salad, house salad." I saw him nod to Stelly. That was their station. "Chicken and dumplings and a shrimp and grits."

"Okay, Brooklynne, the chicken and dumplings, and the shrimp and grits are ours."

We got to work. I demonstrated for her, talking it out as I did each part. She watched and offered ideas along the way.

"What do you think? Are they ready?" I asked her.

"They look amazing."

"Great." I placed them out for the runner. "Next order I'll let you do."

By the time June came in, we had everything prepped for the evening, station cleaned and Brooklynne had gotten to make Balsamic Glazed Salmon. This was our slow time of day, so we only got a hand full of orders. It was either late to lunch or early to dinner folks.

"Well, good evening, y'all. I'm excited to work with you tonight, Brooklynne."

"Yes, ma'am. I'm excited, too."

"You're both in good hands. I'm going to head out."

As I was leaving, Jordan came back to find me.

"There is some girl here asking for you. I think it's that same one as yesterday."

"Riley?"

"Yeah, I think that's what she said her name was."

I groaned. "I'll be right out."

I washed up and then went to find her. She was at the bar. When she saw me, her frown deepened.

"Hi, Jess."

"Riley. What can I do for you?"

"Did you talk to Sawyer yet about me?"

"No, and I'm not. That is between the two of you."

"You're so wrong. I loved him and I just want him back." She stomped her foot.

Not sure why she thinks she loved him. They'd only been dating a few weeks, but what did I know? I wasn't part of their relationship, despite her insisting I get involved.

"I don't think I can do anything for you."

"You won't even try? He would listen to you."

"Look, I am very sorry, but this isn't the place, and this isn't my business to be involved in."

"You're awful! I hate you." She stood up. "You are going to regret pissing me off!"

She then stormed out the front door. All eyes in the place watched her and then turned to look at me. That was too much drama for me. I really think Sawyer dodged a bullet with that one, but she kept telling me I would be sorry. That doesn't bode well for me.

I said goodbye to Cullen, then made my way out the back door. Stepping out, something about my car looked funny.

"Well, bleep!"

I had two flat tires. Stepping closer, it looked like someone cut them. I wanted to curse and scream. Pulling out my phone, I called the police.

"We'll send an officer to your location. Thank you."

"Thanks."

I then sent Sawyer a message.

Me: **Your ex slashed my tires.**

S: **Who? Riley?**

Me: **Yes!**

S: **Do you need me to come up there?**

Me: **No, you're still at work. The police are coming.**

S: **Okay. See you at home.**

I headed back into the building. I wanted to check the security camera and get a copy for the police.

"You're back so soon," Cullen said.

"Yeah, two flat tires. Slashed tires."

"Oh, no!"

"Yeah, can you pull up the camera that faces the back lot?" I asked him.

"Of course."

He clicked until the screen showed the back parking lot. I saw my car on the edge of the lot. Unfortunately, the sun was shining in just the right spot, making the objects on the screen silhouette and hard to tell exactly what was happening.

A dark figure moved from off screen to my car. It was a large male, but I couldn't make out his face. I guess that isn't Riley unless she hired someone to do it.

"Can you put a copy of the footage on this for the police? I think there is an extra USB in that drawer." If these things kept happening, I was going to have to start buying them in bulk. "I'm going to head out to meet the police. Can you bring it out when it's done?"

"Yes, Chef."

I trekked back outside just as a police cruiser pulled into the lot. It was my old friend Kyle Rafferty, but everyone called him Raff.

"Hey, Jess."

"Hey, Raff." I gestured towards my car.

He whistled. "Any ideas?"

"It was a large male, but our security camera didn't get details of his face. The sun was shining right into the lens. Cullen, my new assistant manager, is making a copy for you."

"Thanks. I'll see if Dr. Vega's camera picked anything up." He walked across to the eye doctor. While he was gone, Cullen came out with the thumb drive.

"Thanks. He is across the street at Dr. Vega's."

"It might not have gotten anything because of the angle." He walked over to my car. "Damn, Chef, these are bad. What are you going to do?"

"I have no idea yet. I only have one spare, and that won't get me to the tire shop."

"You can have the one off my car if it helps you get to the tire shop. You can return it once you get the new tire."

"Oh, thanks. I'll let you know."

Rafferty came jogging back. "Okay, not much on his cameras, either. The male kept his back turned, but I got a copy."

I handed him the one we had.

"Thanks. I'll take some pictures and see if I can get fingerprints, then we'll be done."

He got to work. Cullen watched with me for a minute, but then got called inside. I fidgeted and paced while I waited and watched.

Sawyer messaged me.

S: **She's denying it**
Me: **Oh, yeah, sorry. I don't think it was her after all**
S: **Who then?**
Me: **There was a large man on the camera**
S: **Maybe related to Colt**

My pulse quickened as I realized he could be right. *Bleep!* Why were they after me? Was Riley to distract me while the man did that? This was a nightmare.

Me: **It could be**
S: **Well, see you at home soon. Be safe**

Raff finished up. "Do you need help to get new tires? I can call a tow company that does this."

"Really?"

"Yeah, yeah. You remember Elias from back in the day? Runs a shop now. I'll give him a call. What is this, a Toyota?"

"Yeah. Thanks so much."

He waited with me for Elias to come. We made small talk while we waited. Nothing special. After twenty minutes, Elias pulled in.

"Hey, fellow Dashwood Junior High alumni!" Elias yelled, hopping out of his truck. He and Rafferty did the guy-bro handshake-slash-hug thing, then he turned towards me. "Jessie, I haven't seen you in ages. You went off and got famous on us."

"Hi, Elias. Yeah, I guess I did a little." I chuckled. "Thank you for coming out. As you can see, they got me good."

"Yeah, they did, but I'm sure my man, Raff, will figure this out for you."

I smiled, but I had my doubts. Kyle Rafferty was a good enough patrol officer and a good guy, but I had little faith in the police department as a whole. If Chief Stone was doing some corrupt stuff, then it likely trickled down through the entire department.

Elias got to work on the tires, and Raff watched, handing him tools and chatting with him. It was clear they had kept in touch all these years.

He was really quick and within fifteen or so minutes, he had me all set. He even checked the air on the others.

"Now, you'll want to take this in and get it balanced, but you are good for a few days at least," Elias said, wiping his hands on a towel.

"How much do I owe you?"

"No charge at all."

"What? No, I have to pay for the tires at least and for your time. You came all the way out here."

"Someone did you dirty here, I can help out. I'll get some good karma points." He grinned and pointed to the sky. "Just pay it forward or something."

"Well, you always have a free meal here at The Crock Pot. Anything you want."

"Oh, that alphabet soup is the bomb! I could eat a gallon of that."

"Do you want me to get you some to-go?"

"I wouldn't turn it down," Elias said.

"Raff, want anything before you head back?"

"I'd take one of those iced teas."

"Alright, I'll be right back with soup for you and an iced tea."

Minutes later, I had paid with the food, and they were on their way. I was leaving work nearly two hours late, which was going to cut into my evening plans. I headed home with a lot on my mind and my stomach flip-flopping like a gymnast.

Chapter Seventeen

I hurried into the house and straight to the shower. After my rushed shower, I stood staring into my closet for far too long.

"What does one wear to a city council meeting?" I asked Lulu, who was sitting on the bed watching me.

She meowed.

"Black slacks. Good choices." I took them from the hanger, sliding them on. "Now, what shirt?"

She began cleaning herself. I guess she was done helping me. I found a white t-shirt and then a black blazer with thin silver pinstripes.

"This might work." I put on the shirt and jacket, slipped my feet into silver flats and then added a silver and black beaded necklace.

I stood back to look at myself in the mirror. It wasn't half-bad. I should get more clothes like this. My hair was still wet, but it would dry before the meeting.

Sawyer and Vee should be home any second. Then we were going to dinner before the meeting, which starts at seven this evening. I'd heard the meetings can run longer, especially if there were fights. While I hadn't been to one of these meetings, the fights were famous. You can find clips online.

"Honey, we're home!" came Sawyer's deep, playful voice from downstairs.

"Up here," I yelled down.

Their footsteps could be heard coming up and then into my room.

"Wow, don't you look nice," Vee said. "I need to rethink what I was going to wear."

"Why? What were you going to wear?"

"A Neal Barney tee with jeans."

"Oh." Darn, that was a good idea. I should have done that.

"Where do y'all wanna go eat?" Sawyer asked. He always thought about food. Honestly, me too, but more about cooking it.

"I haven't even thought about it."

"Me neither."

"What about Mills Steakhouse?"

"Oh, fancy."

"Ooh, la, la."

"Well, Jess is dressed up and I'll put on a jacket and my nice shoes. It will be great."

"Do we have enough time?" I asked. I felt so guilty being late tonight, but it wasn't like they got home any earlier just because I did.

"Yeah, we should. We'll hurry!"

He jumped up, leaving the room. Vee and I laughed, but then she left to get ready. I was on my own.

Noah sent me a message. He was declining going with me tonight.

N: **April is having a rough day. I'm going to stay with her.**

Me: **I'm sorry to hear. I'll let you know how it goes.**

I checked my reflection once more before heading downstairs to wait for my friends. As usual, Sawyer was the first to join me downstairs.

"Whoa, Mr. Hart, don't you clean up nicely."

He did a few model poses while I cheered him on. When he was done, we had to wait on Vee. It was just a few minutes later. She was wearing a red floral dress with a pale pink shrug. Her hair was actually tame, too.

"Well? What do y'all think?" She twirled for us.

"Gorgeous."

"Lovely.

"Thank you." She did a little curtsy. She was super cute. "Ready to roll?"

"Yep!"

We headed to dinner. It was amazing. I hadn't been to Mills in a long time. It was a staple here in Dashwood, opening in 1970 and run by the same family since.

The décor was what I imagined was prominent back in the early 70s, though I wasn't born then. It had been unchanged my entire life with the dark panel and jewel-colored walls. The lighting was dim and there was outdated artwork on the walls. But it was clean and well kept, so it remained popular with the locals.

"This was a good choice," I said as I finished my last bite of prime rib.

"Very good," Vee said, pushing her plate away.

"So, what's the plan at the city council meeting?" Sawyer asked.

"I don't know yet, but I just want to observe how it goes, how things flow, and the general relationship among the council members."

"Do you know what's on the agenda?"

"No idea. Is that online?"

"Possibly."

Superintendent Rhodes had said I could find information about it online, but I hadn't thought to look for an agenda. We all pulled out our phones and searched. Sawyer found it first.

"Okay, aside from normal housekeeping type stuff, it looks like they will be talking about a vacant building."

"Oh, I bet it's that one out on Jamison Avenue," Vee said.

"Maybe. It doesn't say here. Then they are going to discuss festivals, public safety, transportation, and some federal grant."

"Well, none of that seems related to Colt or the school." I pouted.

"Are we still going?"

"Yeah, I still think we should. I mean, who knows, maybe they will talk about it. Isn't there an 'any new business' thing? Why am I thinking that's a thing?" I asked.

"I have heard of it."

"Yeah, it seems like a thing."

We settled the bill and then headed over to city hall, arriving with about fifteen minutes to spare. The parking lot only had about a dozen cars in it.

"I guess not a lot of people come to these," Vee said.

"That's disappointing." But then, I hadn't thought it important to come until now.

We walked in and found the conference room easily. It was a large room with a stage at the front. There were a dozen small tables with name tents on them, each had a glass of water, and a notepad with a pen. In front of them were rows of chairs for the audience with only six people filling them so far. That left more than half of them empty.

"Where should we sit?" Vee asked.

"In the back would be my vote," I said, frowning.

It wouldn't matter where we sat though, we were going to stick out with so few people here. The meeting would start soon, but I hoped more people would show up. I wanted to blend in.

We took seats in the back row, talking quietly with each other while we waited. Thankfully, a few more people came in and took seats in the audience section. That made me feel a bit better.

"Well, well, well, who do we have here? The three troublemakers from back in the day. Still friends, I see." It was Chief Stone.

"Hello, Chief," Sawyer and I said in almost unison.

"What are you all doing here?"

"Well, as a new business owner in the community, I thought it was time that I got more involved."

"Um, oh-okay." His sarcastic tone was not lost on me.

"Good to see you, too, Chief," I said dismissively.

He gave me a look, then huffed away. I felt like I won a battle, but I knew it was not the end of the war. It would never be the end with Chief Stone. He just had a grudge from years gone by and maybe a little from my dad's crime. He needed to get over my rebellious teen years. I wasn't even that bad.

Council members came in. I recognized the mayor, mayor pro tem, and then a few of the council members. Chief Stone greeted a few. When the Finance Director, Davis Campbell, came in, Chief Stone greeted him. Then they both looked our way.

I could feel my heart up in my throat as it pounded. Perhaps this was a mistake. Would they know I was here because of what Colt had uncovered?

The mayor called the meeting to order and asked the city clerk to do the roll call. Superintendent Van Rhodes was seated at the end. He saw me and frowned, but it gave me hope that perhaps they would discuss the school, and if I was lucky, something with the budget.

Next, it was a consent to the agenda. I have no idea what it meant, but from the way things went, I assume it had to do with approving the agenda items. After that they got into the meat of the meeting. They started with one of the council members introducing her committee, which was looking at the vacant building on Jamison Avenue. Vee is so smart.

"We would like to propose a complete teardown and use the lot as a park." She went through an entire presentation, complete with PowerPoint slides. It was interesting. If I got a vote, I would love to see a park go in there.

That building had been empty since we were kids. It was one of those hangout places for us. We would break in and then go sit up on the roof, watching the world from six stories up. One time, there was a homeless man in there. He chased us out, and we never went back.

Vee and Sawyer looked over at me. Perhaps they were remembering the same night. I smiled at them.

The council members took a vote on the proposal, and it passed with a vote of ten in favor and two not. I wasn't surprised. It was an eyesore.

Next item was the quarterly art festivals. Nothing too exciting, it was just to review the dates for next year. It passed with all twelve approving it. They were more or less the same each year, so of course it passed.

When they got to the public safety part of the agenda, that's when Chief Stone spoke, giving an update on hiring in the department, retirements, and role changes as officers were promoted. Then he addressed some of the petty crime.

"We still don't have a suspect in the murders at the Beck Apartments, but we are getting closer." His eyes locked on me.

A few people turned to look. Finance Director Campbell looked at me as well, his eyes narrowed.

Seriously, it wasn't me. I wanted to scream that, but I just tried to keep a neutral expression and not squirm.

They moved on, but I didn't hear anything else that was said until the end of the meeting when they started to discuss the agenda for the next meeting. They announced that the school budget would be discussed then, along with other boring stuff.

Bleep! I didn't ever want to come back here, but after making a bold statement about being a new business owner to two of the members, I felt obligated.

Sawyer nudged me when I didn't stand right away.

"Sorry, is it over?" I whispered.

"Yeah, you okay?"

"I don't want to talk about it … at least not here." I scanned the room, finding Chief Stone in deep conversation with Davis Campbell. If I used curse words, now would be the time for the big one.

I was so busy watching them that I didn't notice Superintendent Rhodes walk up to me.

"Well, Chef, what did you think about your first council meeting?" Superintendent Rhodes asked.

"Oh, it was interesting." I hope I sounded sincere and calm, even though my heart was beating out of my chest.

"Do you have any questions I can answer?"

"No, it was all pretty straightforward."

"Great. I hope we'll see you next month."

"Yes, of course," I confirmed with a smile.

"Good night." He nodded to the three of us before moving on to someone else.

We quickly left before anyone else talked to us. Back in the car, I sighed.

"I hate that we didn't learn much," Vee said from the back seat.

"Yeah, but what was up with the superintendent talking to you? Have you met him before?" Sawyer asked.

"Oh, I didn't tell you. Yes, the other day I saw him."

"Ah."

"And what was with them all looking at you when they were talking about the Beck apartment murders?" Vee said.

"Right? I wanted to run out."

"Makes me think they are all suspicious," Sawyer said.

"Yeah, me too."

We headed home and stared at the board. It didn't help. I felt no closer to knowing who did this. I wanted to curse Colt for not just telling us, but he didn't actually know either. Just had some ideas. We had all the suspects on the board now.

Thankfully, Sawyer hadn't questioned me when he saw Riley's name. I did notice that there was an exclamation mark added to it in blue ink. A frowny face was added to Duncan Jones's name.

I have no idea who added it, but if I had to guess Vee had done it. Not because she suspected him, but because he was listed at all.

I looked at each name one by one along with the details below.

What did we know? I thought.

The chief was on friendly terms with Davis Campbell, and by the way they both looked at me, they talked often. Superintendent Van Rhodes didn't seem to talk to either of them. There wasn't any talk about the budget, so I hadn't gotten any idea of how that even worked.

Mr. Jones and Shirley Wolfe weren't there, but perhaps they will come when the school budget is on the agenda. I also assumed that some of the other department heads and teachers from the high school would come to that as well, like Ms. Cleary for cosmetology or Mr. Alton for the mechanic shop.

Unfortunately, I won't know for another month. I didn't think I could wait that long to figure out Colt's murder.

Ugh! I wanted to scream.

I rubbed my temples.

"Well, tomorrow is another day," I said. "I'm not going to figure this out tonight."

Chapter Eighteen

"So, you didn't learn *anything* last night?" Noah asked.

"Nothing, except to confirm that Chief Stone and Davis Campbell are familiar with each other."

"Um, what about Superintendent Rhodes? Was he there?"

"Yep, but he didn't share much. They'll talk about the school next month. Though I noticed he didn't really speak to either Chief Stone or Davis Campbell. Not sure if that is relevant, but I noticed it."

"Bummer, but maybe I'll be able to make it then," Noah said.

"I hope so."

"So, what's our next steps?"

"I have no idea. I'm kind of at a loss with this. I stared at that board last night and again this morning. We need more clues or proof."

"Yeah, I'm at a loss, too. We can't very well go right up and accuse them without more proof. Some grainy pictures, screen grabs, and spreadsheets from financial statements aren't much to go on at all. The spreadsheets could be faked. The pictures could be innocent. It is just frustrating." He balled up his fists as he spoke.

I had never known Noah to have a temper, but I knew this was important to him. I wanted to do better to help him solve this, but even with Earl's murder, it was dumb luck that I stumbled into the robbery and then by dropping my phone, the police were called. I might have figured it out, but it was a slow process.

"I'm sorry. I wish I knew what to do."

"I know. It isn't up to you. I just wish the police department was more helpful, but if the chief is involved, I can see why they aren't."

"Did they ever say anything about cameras catching anything?"

"Nothing. The shooter must have known where each was pointed. He or she was standing just outside of the frame and, even worse, seemed to disappear into thin air. Where did they go? Back in the building? Down the alley? No idea because they didn't have stupid cameras in those places."

I thought about meeting Imogen Potter. She had been killed for talking to me, at least that's what Detective Upton had alluded to. He still hadn't confirmed why she was killed. Perhaps, he didn't know.

But I had only spoken to her briefly, so obviously someone nearby had seen me there. Nobody knew I had gone over there unless they saw me or followed me. There was no motive or reason to know I would be there.

Heck, I didn't even put much thought into it, I just sort of drove over there that morning.

I also remembered that man who had bumped into me while we were leaving. It was the day we had packed up Colt's apartment with April. It was possible he lived there and had been watching us. Who knows?

"The person has to be in those apartments," I blurted.

"Why do you say that?"

"Because of poor Ms. Imogen Potter. She died simply from a two-minute conversation with me, well, obviously I don't know that's why she was killed. But nobody would have known that I spoke to her unless they were in that building."

"Um, interesting thought." He sat quietly for a moment. I could almost see his mind turning. "But perhaps she knew more about Colt than we know. Neither of them is still here to share how close they were or weren't."

He had a point there. It is possible that they were good friends, not just neighbors. Look at Sawyer and our neighbors. He often had tea with the nice ladies two doors down. They were one of the few with a front porch and he would often walk down to visit with them. They would spend hours gossiping and sharing stories. He was such a people person. Could Colt and Imogen have been more than casual neighbors? We would never know.

"True." I stood. "Well, time to get ready for the day."

Hours later, it was the end of my shift. Day three for the apprentices. Tonight, we would rotate them again, so that Shayla could have a chance with June tonight. Brooklynne was with Natalie and Jacoby was with Stelly. I wanted them to get a rounded look at how the restaurant works, well as much as I could.

"Alrighty, gang, I'm out. June is the chef tonight."

I had a plan, but I didn't want to tell Noah yet. If I didn't find anything out, it would just get his hopes up. My plan was to swing by the apartment building and just have a look around. Maybe see if any of the neighbors were walking around that I could talk to. Perhaps I could catch a name on the mail slots.

I wasn't sure exactly what I would do yet, but sometimes apartment buildings like that would have a kind of directory. Typically, only the last names. It helped with deliveries and mail. I could then look up the names against any connected to anyone on the city council, or maybe even that company that Ralph found that owns the bank account.

When I got near the building, I noticed a large police presence around it.

"What the bleep?" I slowed and moved into an empty parking spot a block away. I sat in the car, trying to see what was going on. I couldn't tell from here.

Detective Upton wouldn't like it, but I got out and walked closer. There were a lot of people standing nearby watching, too. Maybe I could blend in.

"What happened?" An older gentleman asked someone else standing nearby.

"Another dead body," the other man said.

"This block is getting so dangerous."

"Do we know who it was?"

"Some guy in the Beck Apartments. Same place as the last two."

"You won't catch me in that place."

"I hear he had only been living there a few months."

I listened to the crowd as they mumbled and discussed the block. This was some turn of events. I wish I knew who the man was. If I could get a peek at him, I would know if it was the man who threatened me.

I moved a little closer, but still trying to blend in with the crowd. As I neared the entrance of the apartments, I could see them rolling out a stretcher with a body covered on it.

Bleep! No chance of seeing him.

Then Detective Upton came out behind the stretcher, along with Officer Rafferty and Officer Roberts. I ducked my head a bit and moved back behind a tall man.

"Chef Jessica?" Rafferty called out.

Busted. I guess the tall man wasn't tall enough to hide me.

"Um, oh, hey." I moved forward. My face warmed when I saw Detective Upton's face as he moved next to Raff.

"What are you doing over here?" Detective Upton asked.

"Oh, I was just driving to a friend's house down that way and saw all this." Would he buy my lie?

Officer Rafferty smirked and turned away from us. He began talking to some bystanders. Maybe getting witness statements, but I couldn't hear him as I was under the wrathful stare of the detective. I guess I hadn't fooled Raff, but then again, we knew each other from childhood.

He stared at me before speaking again. "I'm going to believe you, because you will remember I told you to avoid coming this way. Right?"

"Yes, of course. I mean, I was just driving past, not going here." I smiled, then lowered my voice. "I am sure you can't tell me, but does this have to do with Colt?"

"It seems you already know that I can't."

"You can't blame for trying."

He looked around, then looked at me. "This is all I will say, and I need you to actually hear me this time, you shouldn't come to this block again, not until we get this solved."

That sounded like confirmation that this was related to Colt's murder.

"Alrighty, well, I will get on out of here now. I'll go the long way to my friend's house next time."

He looked at me suspiciously but didn't say anything. We both turned away from each other, me to leave and him to get back to work.

Back at my car, I fought the panic bubbling up in my chest. This was getting scary. Three dead bodies in the same building, possibly all related. Either that or the neighbors were right. The block was just dangerous.

Also, I hadn't learned anything about that man who threatened me. Now, he was likely dead. What did that mean? Had he failed "his boss" or something?

I started to drive off when I noticed there was a note on my windshield. My mind said get out and grab it, but then I remembered a story circulating around a few years ago. It suggested that people would do that to lure you out of your car and then they'd rob you. I have no idea if it was true or not, but why tempt fate?

I left it and drove away, checking my mirrors as I did. I took the long way around to the grocery store. Still in a paranoid state, I scanned the parking lot for a good spot.

There is a camera. I angled into a spot that was right in front of it. Before all of this with Earl and Colt, I never thought much about the security cameras. Now I looked for them, especially with all that was going on.

I climbed out, snatched the note, shoving it into my pocket as I walked quickly to the entrance. With a cart in hand, I started my shopping and tried not to think of the note just yet.

"Hi, Chef," a random shopper called out.

"Chef, we were out to The Crock Pot the other night. Excellent," another said, passing me.

"Those new biscuits are fabulous!"

"Yes, those biscuits are heavenly," a nearby shopper added.

I smiled. It is weird to be almost a celebrity in town. It made me chuckle a bit. It wasn't like I was the only chef in town. This was a foodie town. They mostly knew me from the television competitions I'd been on. I used that to my advantage when it came to my restaurant, too.

I was glad to hear that people liked the addition of the biscuits. We had been getting great feedback on them. I gave Parker a bonus for the suggestion. He deserved it.

Once I'd selected a variety of vegetables and some nice pork, I made my way to the checkout. Tonight would be stir-fry pork with veggies over rice. I had the rice already at home.

The cashier was chatty, asking me about my dinner plans, and asking about the restaurant. It was polite and distracted me from thinking about the note shoved in my pocket. It was burning a hole in my pocket, but depending on what it said, I wanted to read it in the safety of my own home.

As I was walking out, I saw a familiar face.

"Shirley? Oh, hi." That's weird. I haven't seen her in years, but now I was seeing her everywhere.

"Jessie, hi! Wow, is it my imagination or am I seeing a lot of you lately?"

"Ha, yeah, I was thinking the same. Good to see you."

"You too. Picking up something for dinner?"

"Yes, pork stir fry. You?"

"Dinner for one, so probably a microwave dinner or something."

"Ah, well, I better get going. It was good to bump into you."

"You too, Jess, and I'll be stopping by the restaurant soon."

With that awkward interaction out of the way and groceries in hand, I made my way home. Again, I checked my mirrors for any followers or danger. Nothing looked out of place, but would I even know if someone was following me? Last time it happened, they made sure I knew.

I arrived safely at home.

"Thank you, Jesus." I muttered a quick prayer. I grabbed my things and headed in.

Setting the groceries on the island, I took a deep breath and then pulled the note from my pocket.

STOP ASKING QUESTIONS OR YOU'RE NEXT

Well, bleepity, bleep, bleep.

What do I do now?

Chapter Nineteen

My roommates got home as I was starting to cook the pork. Rice was in the pot and all the vegetables had been cut to perfection. I focused all my panic into cutting them. I probably overdid it and cut far too many, but oh well, it helped me process my fear.

"Hey, honey, we're home." Sawyer ran to me. "Yum, stir-fry."

"Yeah, I thought you might like it."

"Did you have a good day?" Vee asked. She took a seat at the island.

"Oh, yeah, it was … okay."

"What happened?"

I stirred the pork once before pulling it out, setting it aside while I cooked the veggies, giving a few stirs before turning to face my roommates.

"Okay, so after work, I drove over to Colt's old apartment building, and you won't believe what I found."

"What?!" Vee asked eagerly.

"The police were there. Apparently, there was another murder."

"Holy moly!" they both said.

"Yeah, and even though Detective Upton couldn't tell me details, he said I shouldn't come over there again. That likely means it was related." I paused, stirring the veggies again before continuing. "Which leads me to what happened next."

"What?"

"What happened?"

"I found a note on my car." I pulled it out of my pocket, passing it to them.

They read it and then looked up at me, then read it again.

"This is … wow."

"Did you call the detective?"

"I didn't think to. Should I?"

"Yes!" they yelled.

"Fine. Let me just finish this." I dropped the pork and sauce into the veggies, stirring it in then while that cooked for a few minutes, I grabbed my phone and hit the button for Detective Upton.

"This is Detective Upton."

"Hi, Detective. This is Jessica Vasquez."

"Hi, Jess. If this is about the murder at Beck Apartment, like I said, I can't give you any information."

"No, it's different. Well, related in a way, but different. After I left, I found a threatening note on my car."

"Really? What did it say?"

"Stop asking questions or you're next."

"Good advice. Stop doing that."

"I haven't." The lies were getting easier to tell.

"Uh-huh. I am going to try really hard to believe you, but I know it's a lie. I can come by to pick up the note. Are you free now?"

"Yes. We'll be here all night."

"Great. I'll be over in about fifteen." I heard a tiny voice in the background yelling, Dad. "It might be twenty, but I'll be there."

"Okay. Thanks."

We hung up and I turned to face my friends.

"He is going to come get it soon. Why don't y'all go change and we can eat? Maybe we'll be able to finish before he gets here."

They nodded and headed upstairs.

I plated dinner onto three plates, setting it on our table. Then fixed drinks, grabbed silverware and I was just finishing up when they both came back down.

Twenty minutes later, we had finished eating. Sawyer was cleaning up when there was a knock at the door.

"Hi, Detective. Oh, Aiden, right?" I asked when I opened the door to find Detective Upton with his son.

"You remembered. Yes, Brooke was nursing Evie, and it was easier for me to just bring him. I figured it would be okay, right?" He smiled awkwardly.

"Yeah, it's fine. Come in."

Vee came forward to greet Aiden. She loved children.

"Do you like teddy bears?" She handed him one. "This is Freddy Bear."

Aiden smiled and reached for the bear. By the look on Aiden's face, Vee was not going to get to keep that one as Freddy Bear was likely going home with Aiden Upton.

"Would you like a drink?" I offered.

"No, thanks. May I see the note?"

He got right to business, I thought.

I walked to the kitchen island and picked up the note, handing it over to him. He read it. It was straightforward. Nothing that could give away who it was from. It was written in bold, dark nearly perfect block letters. Nothing distinctive about it, at least to my amateur eye.

"Okay, this is good. I will take this into our forensics tomorrow to see if we can pull any prints or get a handwriting expert to review it. Thank you."

He looked over at his son, who was happily playing with Vee. Sawyer had joined them, too. They had Aiden belly laughing, as they had Freddy Bear talking. It was cute.

"Your friends are nice."

"They are."

"Please be careful out there, okay? I know you want to find your friend's killer. I do, too." He exhaled, running his hand over his face. "I keep thinking I'm getting close, but then my clues seem to dissolve. Finger prints go missing, witnesses recant their statements. It is almost like someone is working against me in solving this."

"Really?"

I had some ideas about that, but I couldn't share just yet. I thought of the clue board in the other room. Should I show it to him, or would he think it was crossing the line?

"Yeah, I thought it was being sleep deprived. Between him and Evie, plus the stressful job, I am not sleeping much."

"I'm sorry."

Another good reason for me not to have children. I liked my sleep. Good for those that had them. They are cute, but again, sleep better.

"But, and I can't stress this enough, please stop poking at this. With three dead bodies at the same apartment, this seems connected to something that I don't need spreading." He tapped the note on the kitchen island. "Like this."

"Yeah, I get it. I'm just trying to help."

He exhaled. The stress was apparent as he seemed to age ten years right before my eyes. I felt a bit bad to be causing trouble for him.

"I get it, Jess, I really do, but my job is to protect this town and the people in it. It makes it more difficult when one of those people keeps seeking out trouble."

"I'm sorry." I didn't know what else to say.

He looked at me for a second, before forcing a smile.

"Well, we'll get out of here. Gotta get this little guy home for bath and bed," he said in a dad voice.

"No bed!" Aiden yelled.

"Come on, little buddy. I'll walk you out," Sawyer offered.

He put out his hand. Little Aiden took it and happily skipped along with his new friend and Freddy Bear tucked under one arm. Vee smiled, watching him leave.

"You okay with letting the bear go?" I asked.

"Yeah, Aiden is a cutie-patootie." She smiled.

With that bit of business done, we settled in for our normal evening television watching. I scrolled through social media sites and then once I was bored with that, I played a word game.

I guess I fell asleep playing my game because I woke up a few hours later. The television was on, but Vee and Sawyer weren't in the living room any longer.

I stretched and went to the kitchen for a glass of water. As I was turning to head upstairs, a strange noise from the nearby window caught my attention. It was a tapping noise. I assumed it was that black and white cat. They liked to come to the window sometimes to look at Lulu.

I crept towards it, sinking low, trying to peek out. As I got near it, I could hear a distinct scratching sound that did not sound like a cat. My blood froze and my heart thumped in my throat. Despite that, I pushed the curtain slightly to peer out into the near darkness.

Still expecting to see the cat, I was startled to see a man's face move into view. It was too dark to identify him, but I knew what I saw. His eyes seemed to lock with mine. He cursed and pulled something up to the window.

Oh, bleep! It's a gun!

I let out a blood-curdling scream and fell to the floor as shots rang out above me, thankfully, missing me. Then I heard an engine roar and tires squeal. Sawyer came running down the stairs with a metal bat in hand, swinging it. I could hear Vee on the phone, possibly with 9-1-1.

I lay on the floor, trying to catch my breath and restart my heart.

"Are you okay?" he asked, coming to check on me.

"Yeah, I think so," I stammered.

"What happened?" He walked to the window, peeking out. "Did someone try to shoot you?"

"I think that was their plan, yes," I said from the floor.

My body was shaking, and I felt weak. I was struggling to sit up. That was the scariest thing that's happened to me. Aside from the time I was held at gunpoint and knocked around by robbers in my restaurant.

Okay, maybe that was scarier.

But this one happened at my home, my safe place. It didn't feel so safe at the moment. I put my hand across my chest. I could feel my heart beating.

Time passed slowly as I relived the events. Finally, the police arrived, statements were given, and forensics collected evidence. They called an ambulance, but I declined going to the hospital. They gave first aid which was mostly pulling glass out of my skin and cleaning the wounds. They said I should be fine.

"You should be okay, though watch for infection and you should follow up with your regular doctor," the EMT said. "They might want to start you on an antibiotic and maybe give you something for pain."

"Thanks," I mumbled.

It was hours before everyone left, and we were able to go to sleep. We had a patch over the window, but the landlord said he'd get it fixed in the morning.

"You going to be okay?" Vee asked.

"I think so." Honestly, I didn't know.

"Want me to sleep with you?"

"No, no, that's okay. It's only a couple of hours before we have to get up for work."

She nodded before going to her room.

Sawyer hugged me, kissed my head, then quietly walked away. I know he was worried about me, but what could we do? This now seemed to be my life.

That's when I realized that Noah could be in danger, too. It was too early to text, but I wanted to warn him. Should I email him? Send the text anyway?

I laid in bed, staring at the ceiling. If he knew that I could be in danger, he would warn me.

Me: **Sorry if this wakes you, but someone tried to break in and shoot me tonight.**

His reply came almost instantly.

N: **Holy crap. You okay?**

Me: **Yes, I'm okay. They missed.**

N: **Oh, good.**

Me: **I just wanted to let you know, just in case**

N: **Warning received. Thanks. If you want me to call Parker to fill in for you, let me know**

Me: **No, no, work will distract me**

N: **Okay, get some sleep if you can**

Me: **You too! Why are you awake?**

N: **Nightmares. All good now.**

Me: **Sorry to hear. See you tomorrow.**

I felt better letting him know. I would have felt so much guilt if I hadn't. Now if I could just get a few hours of sleep, but I had a feeling I was up for the day.

Chapter Twenty

I slept for maybe another hour after the police left, but it was mostly tossing and turning. My mind kept replaying the man's face, and the gun pointed at me. The sound of the gun firing overhead would haunt me forever. It echoed in my ears like the worst kind of earworm.

I slumped my way around my morning routine, then yawned my way to work. I should have taken Noah up on calling Parker in to take my shift, but I really wanted to keep things normal.

"Oh, Jess, you okay?" Noah asked when I went into the office to drop my stuff.

"I'm okay, I think." I plopped down in a chair with a heavy sigh.

"No, really? You probably should have taken the day to relax and rest. I have Parker on standby."

"Oh, no, no, I should be … well, I'm tired and that was scary, but I think working will be a nice distraction."

He studied me for a moment, then nodded.

"If you're sure."

"Yeah. Tell him to relax."

Noah pulled out his phone and typed out a message.

"Okay, done." He looked at me. "So, any idea who it was?"

"No, none. But if the note I received yesterday is any indication, it was a threat related to Colt's murder."

"Wait? What note?"

"Oh, I didn't tell you." I paused. How much should I share? I guess all of it. I filled him in on my plan to find the man who threatened me after we cleaned out Colt's apartment.

"Okay, hold up? How many times have you been threatened because of this?"

"I guess, once at his apartment, another with the note, and then at my house with the gun." Plus, all the times Riley has warned me, but I wasn't sure that was related. Or was it? "I guess my tires being slashed was another warning."

"I thought we were doing this together."

"We are, but you have been preoccupied with April, which I completely understand, by the way. She needs you. But it hasn't left us as much time to work together. Plus, you are grieving for your friend. I thought I could do some of this without you."

"Fair enough. Go on." He gestured for me to tell him everything I've done.

I continued to fill him in on the events that have been happening. There wasn't much I hadn't already told him, so I mostly just went back through everything from the start, even the stuff he already knew.

"And that brings us to last night with the gunman."

"Yikes, well, I know Colt and he wouldn't want to put us in danger, so maybe we just stop."

"No, I mean it is scary, but I feel like the threats are coming hard now, so I must be close to the answer."

Who was I? I shouldn't be so casual about a murder, but I felt determined, and I wanted to figure it out before anyone else was killed.

"Maybe, but that makes it even scarier," he said.

"But wouldn't it be nice to have justice for Colt, for his family? Heck, for you."

He flashed me a weak smile.

"This has been harder than I thought it would be. I have been trying to be okay and strong, mostly for April. But being around his family so much, I keep expecting him to walk in with his booming, jolly voice. Yet, I know he isn't. It sucks," he hung his head.

"I'm sorry."

It sounded hollow in my ears, but the sentiment was sincere. I simply didn't know what else to say. There were no magic words to erase grief. Grief had to heal and ease with time, and even if it was still there, it wasn't so raw.

We sat in silence for a few minutes, but this time there were no tears. After a few minutes, we got to work. No other words were said or needed at this point.

The day overall was normal and boring. Boring was good at this point. We were busy, but nothing we couldn't handle at this point. We had been open for five months now. It was going well, and I had a strong team. If only I could settle into some kind of boring in my personal life.

"Chef, that chick is back again."

"Really? What is her deal?" I groaned. "Tell her I'll be right there."

I washed my hands. As I stared at the water washing over my hands, I thought how unbelievably tired I was. Too tired to deal with whatever this girl wanted. She had become quite a thorn in my side.

"Hi, Riley. What's up?" I tried to keep my tone neutral, but I was annoyed as heck.

"Why do you have such a problem with me?"

"Me with you? You're stalking me at my place of business."

"You told Sawyer that I slashed your tires! What the hell?"

"You keep coming up here harassing me and then I leave to find my tires slashed. What was I supposed to think?"

"I'm not a bad person." Tears formed in her eyes.

I instantly felt awful, but at the same time, she was coming to me all these times. If anyone was going to cry, it should be me.

"Look, I am sorry. I was wrong about that, but you need to let Sawyer go. You weren't going out with him long, so why are you so ... clingy?"

Her mouth fell open. I guess I hit a nerve.

"I'm not ... clingy. He is just such a ... great guy. I never meet that kinda guy anymore."

I couldn't argue with that. Sawyer was one of the good ones.

"Yes, he is, but he ended it because you were rude to me. There is one thing about Sawyer. He is a loyal person."

"Yeah." She wiped a tear that slid down her face. "I mean you know how hard it is to date, right? You of all people should know how hard it is out there for singles, especially after your most recent dating experience."

Oh, this girl. I took a breath, counting to ten before speaking. I let her comment go. She clearly didn't understand what she was saying wrong. Some people are just clueless.

"Look, I need to get back to work, but is this over? Are you going to keep coming here?"

"No, no, I'm done. You win. Sawyer is yours."

"We're just friends."

"If you say so, but he picked you over me."

"We have been friends for thirty-odd years. Only friends. I promise."

"Whatever." She flipped her hair and stomped out.

I really hoped that was the last interaction with her. She's crazy. Sawyer dodged a bullet. No matter how good she was at his zombie-fighting video game, she was looney.

I got back to work. The apprentices arrived shortly after, so I did a quick check-in to see how things were going. They were all enthusiastic and thriving. The rest of the staff gave rave reviews of them.

"They are hard workers."

"Shayla is creative and going to be a great asset."

"We have to keep them."

I chuckled as I thought about it, and I couldn't wait to give a report to Mr. Jones. He would be so proud.

Once June came in, I passed the torch of the executive chef to her for the night. I was ready for a long, long nap.

Heading to the office, I grabbed my purse and said good night to Cullen. Noah had left a little early today to make a drop at the bank and he was having dinner with Colt's family.

When I stepped out into the bright sun and humid air, I squinted. I should have pulled my sunglasses out already. I began fishing in my purse for them.

Got'em!

As I settled the sunglasses on my face, I hit the unlock button on my key fob. There was a sudden burst of hot, white fire and the blast knocked me to the ground, nearly flat on my back. There was a burning sensation from my head to my toes.

I tried to move, but the pain shot through me. I was able to lift my head a few inches to see my body. My ears were ringing, and my head was pounding.

What the bleep? Looking down, I was covered in blood. *Holy heck.*

It took my brain a moment or two to realize why I was covered in blood. My car exploded. I stared at the flaming ball of shiny blue metal. I loved that car, and I've had it for ten years.

Bleep!

I laid my head back as a crowd started to form around me. Someone was yelling to call 9-1-1 while Parker and Marco attended to me. I couldn't quite hear what they were saying, but suddenly there were towels and they were cleaning me up.

"Chef, Chef, can you hear me?" Parker asked.

"Yeah." My throat was on fire and I'm not sure if they heard me, so I tried again.

"Don't try to speak. It's okay," he said, wiping my face gently with a damp towel. "Should we give her some water?"

"Not yet. Let's wait for the EMTs." Marco said.

There were sirens coming in the distance, or so it seemed, because within a second there was an EMT by my side and police officers taking statements. The sirens still sounded so far away. I looked around, confused. My mind couldn't seem to focus.

It felt as if I was a spectator and not the patient as they took vitals and assessed my injuries. They were asking Parker and Marco questions, then loaded me onto a stretcher and into the ambulance.

Noah climbed in with me. I was relieved to have a familiar face among the strangers, but I have no idea when he came outside or if I asked him to come with me. He was just there. Still, I was thankful to have him along.

As the doors were shut, I saw Detective Upton stepping out of his car. He looked my way with a frown. The doors shut, and we were off. I tried to focus on what was being said around me. It helped having Noah there to answer some of the questions.

They hooked me to an IV and put some medicine into it. The world blurred as I drifted in and out of consciousness. One of the EMTs kept trying to ask me questions, but I couldn't hear them. Everything sounded distorted, both close and far away at the same time. I tried speaking, but my throat burned.

"This should make you feel better, Chef," one of the EMTs said, or at least that's what I think they said. It was a little fuzzy.

Noah squeezed my hand as the world faded.

I woke up later in a strange place and in screaming pain. Looking around, I saw Sawyer and Vee dozing in chairs next to me. Granny Ines and Aunt Rita were across the room on pull out cots.

I didn't see Noah.

I scanned the room, looking for a clock, so I could see the time, but no clock. Sighing, I laid my head back again.

The door to the room opened and in came a nurse. She went to the monitors, made some notes, then smiled at me.

"How are you feeling? How's your pain?"

"I'm okay. Pain is ... painful." My throat was raw, and my voice sounded gravely in my own ears. How did I sound to her?

"On a scale of one to five, with five being the worst, where would you say your pain is?"

My brain was so foggy, and it was hard to focus on the question. I was still trying to process where I was and what had happened.

"Um, I guess a three or no, four." I tried to move. "Strike that — five."

She nodded, making a note.

"Would you like some water or juice?"

"Yes, please."

My friends and family started to stir, but they didn't say anything. Granny came over, taking my hand while the nurse finished up. She made some adjustments to the IV and then said she would be back in a moment.

"Oh, Jessie, how are you? We were so scared," Granny said once the nurse was gone.

"What happened?" I asked.

"You don't remember?"

"No." But then the flashback started. It was a blurry memory. "Oh, wait, my car. A blast."

"Yes. It's a total loss."

Tears sprung to my eyes. I won that car in a cooking competition years ago. They normally gave cash prizes and trophies or plaques, but this one was special. It was a brand-new car. I'd never owned a new car before that. It had been my most treasured prize. Now it was gone.

"What about me? What did they say?"

"Your injuries are mostly on the surface. Burns and abrasions."

"And a concussion," Sawyer added.

That explained my headache.

"Do they know anything?"

"No, not yet. The detective is checking security cameras. He said he would come visit you in the morning."

"What time is it?"

"Around eleven p.m.," Granny said. "They brought you in around four. You've been asleep since."

"Well, that's not good, right?"

"They said you were in a lot of pain, and it wasn't that unusual with the pain medicine they gave you that you would sleep."

"Was anyone else hurt?"

"No, just you, but some of the other cars in the lot were damaged. It is going to be a lot of cleanup."

I simply nodded as I became drowsy again. I had more questions, but sleep overtook me. Granny whispered she loved me as I fell asleep again.

The next morning, I wasn't in quite as much overall pain as last night, but now it was more centralized to the burns and scrapes. My throat was still sore, but my voice wasn't as hoarse.

The nurse came to apply some topical medicine. She tried to explain it, but my brain was still groggy.

Sawyer and Vee had to go to work, but Granny and Aunt Rita stayed with me. The doctor came after breakfast to assess my progress.

"You'll likely be discharged later today," he said, then left.

"Well, that was ... um ... informative." I chuckled.

"Yeah, the nurses are the real heroes here." Aunt Rita chuckled.

"That's why they have that lovely rose garden dedicated to them by city hall."

"It is lovely." I thought back to just a week before when I was there.

We sat playing cards and chatting while we waited for me to be discharged. From time to time, a nurse would come in to check on me, ask about my pain level, or check my burns. It wasn't fun and they hurt like heck, but I was alive, and it could have been much worse.

"A car is replaceable, mija. You are not," Granny said, hugging me.

"Yeah, I know, but I loved that car. I won that car."

"It was a beautiful car," Aunt Rita said.

Chapter Twenty-One

Yesterday, I'd been discharged from the hospital after a two day stay. My house looked like a gift shop or a florist. There were roughly a dozen floral arrangements all around the townhouse. Plus, a few fruit baskets and self-care style gift baskets.

Then there were all the get well cards, including one from Superintendent Van Rhodes. When I saw that, I wanted to gag. He didn't even know me.

With my discharge, I'd been given strict orders to rest and limit my screen time. Plus, there was wound care. I had to keep them dry and clean, and they gave me a cream to apply.

The burns were a combination of friction burns from sliding across the concrete and then thermal burns from the fire. Thankfully, they were first- and second-degree burns, though mostly the latter.

My body was sore, and it felt as if I'd been roasted and beaten, then forced to run a marathon. They said it was from getting knocked to the ground and from the heat of the car fire.

Putting on my sunglasses, just before the car exploded, had helped protect my eyes, but I'd breathed in some of the hot air and so my throat and lungs had some irritation.

My head was still pounding, which is why I had been told to limit any screen time. That meant no phone, games, and very little television.

It was going to make the days long, but I was sleeping on and off. Plus, Aunt Rita was here to keep me company and take care of me.

We played a few hands of cards together and had a nice visit. She was sweet to take care of me, bringing me drinks and ordering us lunch in.

"Okay, Jessie, are you set until Sawyer and Vee get home?" she asked.

"Yes, I think I can manage anything that comes up from here."

"Oh, what do you need?"

I chuckled softly. "I have water, my phone for emergencies, and the TV remote. I am good."

"If you're sure?"

"I am. Plus, they'll be home soon, but thank you so much."

"I am just so thankful you're okay. We would not know how to live without our Jessie." She leaned over, kissing my head softly.

I tried not to wince at her loving gesture, but with most of my body covered in scrapes, burns, or bruises, there weren't many spots that weren't sore.

"Aw, I love you, Auntie Rita."

"I love you, too." She picked up her purse but kept her eyes on me. What did she think I was going to do, disappear? "Okay, you're good. Yes, you are okay."

"Are you convincing yourself or me?"

"I think both. I'm sorry. You are the closest I had to having a child, and I just love you."

"I know. I love you, too."

"Okay, I'm leaving. Really." She smiled, waved, and awkwardly walked out the front door. She had a key, and I heard her lock it behind her.

My roommates should be home in about an hour. That should give me time for a quick nap. I snuggled down further into the couch, pulling my blanket tighter around me. My head was a bit foggy. A nap should help clear the cobwebs.

I was startled awake almost exactly an hour later.

"Hey. How're feeling?" Vee asked.

"Um, not bad." I yawned and stretched.

"Are you up for a visitor today?" Sawyer asked.

"I don't know. Who is it?"

"Don't get mad, but I talked to Riley. She really wants to apologize for harassing you and explain."

"Sawyer, I love you, but I'm not ready to face her."

"I understand, but after having a heart to heart with her, I know she feels awful. She has a lot of insecurities, and she wants to ensure you know she was not involved in this."

"Fine." I sighed, laying back down. I was too tired to argue with him.

"Are you sure?" He reached for my hand, squeezing it.

"I'm tired. I feel like I was hit by a car, but I'm okay to talk to her."

"Okay, I'll call her."

He walked away. We could hear him in the other room talking, but not what he was saying.

"Are you sure you're okay with her coming?" Vee whispered.

"No, but I have a feeling I should just get it over with." I paused. "So, when did all this happen with Sawyer and Riley?"

"Today. They met for lunch, and he hasn't stopped talking about her since."

"Gag."

"Actually, I think it's sweet, and perhaps we were too quick to judge her."

"Really?" I sat up slightly to look at Vee. She was smiling.

"Yeah, I talked to her for a minute. She seems really sorry about everything."

I sighed, closing my eyes. I wasn't going to fight, but I really didn't want to hear her apology. She'd been a thorn in my side for days and almost each time she'd leave, something strange would happen. The last being my car blowing up.

How could I get over that? But remembering what Detective Upton had said about the security footage, maybe Riley wasn't involved.

Detective Upton had come to see me at the hospital. He'd let me know that they had reviewed our security cameras plus Dr. Vega's eye clinic's footage. They saw the same sized figure on the day my tires had been slashed.

"We are completely sure it was the same person as they pick the time that the sun is brightest, almost like they know that the cameras can't see them well then."

"That's strange."

"Yeah, but we are checking at the other businesses nearby as well, to see what we can find. I promise we will catch this person."

"And you looked into Riley Harding?"

"Yes, I did. She was there, but there was no sign that she went near the back parking lot and after questioning her, I have no reason to suspect her."

I sighed. He'd left me after that. It was frustrating that they couldn't solve any of these issues. He seemed just as frustrated. I tried to be understanding, but wasn't this his job?

Sawyer came back into the room. The smile on his face was telling. He was clearly into this girl. I had to forgive her.

"Okay, she's on her way and said she would stop to pick up some dinner. I said Sushi 73 would be easy. I hope that was okay."

"It's perfect," I said.

"Great. I'm going to change before she gets here." He leaned over, kissing the top of my head softly. "I really hope you both can make up."

"I'll try." I smiled at him.

"Thanks, friend."

"I'm going to change, too, but do you need anything before I go?"

"No, I'm set, but I think I'm going to get up for a minute. Run to the restroom."

Several minutes later, we were all back in the living room waiting for Riley. I still was on the fence about how I felt about her, but I'd resolved myself to at least hear her out, for Sawyer.

There was a knock. Sawyer popped up.

"Hey, come in."

"Thanks. I brought dinner." She handed him the bag. She walked over to the couch where I was sitting. "Hi, Jess. How are you feeling?"

Her tone was sweet and calm. Not the edgy one from her trips to The Crock Pot.

"I'm doing better."

"Thank you for letting me come talk to you." She looked over to the kitchen where Sawyer was unpacking dinner. "Should we eat first or talk first?"

"We can talk first," I said, flatly. I really didn't want to hear what she had to say, but I would for Sawyer and for Vee, who now seemed like she was on team Riley.

"Okay. I just want to say how very sorry I am for … well, everything. I really shouldn't have come to your restaurant. I was feeling insecure, unwanted." She took a deep breath. "It is childhood trauma."

A tear slid down her face. Ugh, she was going to play to my empathic side. *Dang it.* My weak spot.

"I can understand that. It is hard to trust after … stuff," I said.

"Yeah, but I'm going to try to not let it get in my way. Sawyer and I talked. He is willing to give me a second chance, but only if you will forgive me."

I looked over at Sawyer. He tried not to make eye contact with me but flashed me a weak smile. Of course, he threw me under the bus. He might be a loyal friend, but sometimes he didn't want to be a bad guy, ever.

"Yeah, it's fine. Just tell me this, do you know who did this to me? I mean, it didn't have anything to do with your visits, right? My tires and then my car."

"No, not me at all." She held her hands up in defense. "I promise."

Studying her, I tried to decide what I thought. She seemed sincere.

"Okay, thanks. I didn't think so, but I had to ask."

"Does that mean we're good?"

"Yeah, we're good." I smiled.

"Well, okay. Thank you." She clapped her hands together, then started to lean forward, stopping herself. Thank goodness that she didn't hug me. I might be okay forgiving her, but only so far.

"So, y'all ready to eat?" Vee asked.

We went to the table where Sawyer had laid everything.

"This looks great, Riley. Thank you," I said. "Sushi 73 is my favorite."

"That's what Sawyer said. It was a little bit to butter you up."

I looked at her and then smiled. "Well, it worked."

Sawyer passed me the spicy tuna bowl that she got for me. "I told her it was your favorite."

"Oh, it is. If Kano ever stops making this, I will be sad."

Kano was the chef and owner at Sushi 73. We had become friends years ago at a cooking competition. We clicked being from the same hometown.

He knew just what I liked to eat, too. After he'd opened Sushi 73, he would see me coming and start making my bowl.

He had come into my restaurant, too, and loved my alphabet soup. He would get it with half a turkey club sandwich.

We continued to eat and make small talk. Now that I was getting to know her without the weirdness between us, she was actually fun. Her quick wit matched Sawyer's, and I could barely keep up with their banter.

My head started to spin a bit and the yawns began.

"Y'all are a riot! I am having fun." I laughed through a yawn. "But I'm sorry. I need to rest."

"Do you need help?" Vee asked.

"No, no. I'm going to take my pain meds and then head up to bed. Good night, all." I waved and went to bed.

Lying in bed, I thought about Riley and Sawyer. I really hoped that she wasn't involved, because after this evening, I liked her. I fell asleep with that thought in my head.

Chapter Twenty-Two

Day five stuck at home, but who's counting? At least I had people to help me or check on me. Like today, Mr. Jones wanted to check on me and we were going to discuss the students.

Until he got here, I relaxed and let my aunt wait on me. She made it her mission to ensure I rested and didn't move except to go to the bathroom.

"Where do you think you're going, young lady?" She snapped.

"To the bathroom."

"Do you need help?"

"Um, I think I can handle it." I laughed.

"Well, I'll come wait outside the bathroom for you."

I didn't want to fight with her, so I just let her walk with me to the half bathroom, then when I came out, she escorted me back to the couch.

Every five minutes, she'd pepper me with questions.

"Do you need a drink? Do you need something to eat? Want another blanket?"

"I'm good. I still have water. I'm not hungry. No, this one is fine."

Mr. Jones was going to be a nice change of pace and give her someone else to interact with than just me. I wish Granny Ines was able to come over, but she volunteered at a nursing home and did a lot with her church group.

She checked on me each day. Honestly, though, I think she was glad Aunt Rita had something to do besides hang around their house. Since she'd sold her dance studio, she hadn't found a hobby or things to keep her busy. She'd sometimes volunteer with Granny, but otherwise, she didn't do much.

After lunch, there was a knock at the door.

Aunt Rita held a hand up for me to stay while she hopped up to answer the door.

"Hello, Duncan, please come in."

"Hi, Rita. It's so good to see you." He kissed her check as they hugged hello.

I peeked over the couch as he came over.

"Hi, Jessie. These are for you from the kids and me." He held out a floral arrangement and a stack of cards. "It looks like you have quite a few people thinking of you."

"Oh, thank you. These are beautiful and I will look through the cards later," I said, taking them from him. I set them on the end table behind me.

"How are you feeling?"

"I'm feeling okay. Sore and the burns are still a bit raw, but overall, I'm okay."

"Duncan, may I get you a drink?" Aunt Rita asked.

"Maybe hot tea?"

"With sugar or sweetener?"

"Sugar is perfect."

"Of course." She left us.

He took a seat across from me on the couch.

"So, what exactly happened?"

"Not exactly sure." I didn't want to tell him *exactly* what was going on. "They are still investigating what happened to it. Maybe faulty wiring."

"That's a shame. Didn't you win that car?"

"I did. I'll miss it very much."

"So, down to business. How are my kiddos doing?"

"They are doing great. Exceeding expectations. Natalie cannot say enough good things about Shayla."

"Natalie is your pastry chef, correct?"

"That's right."

"Shayla has talked almost non-stop about it. She has been giving lessons to the rest of the class, and everyone is excited, hoping for their turn."

"Well, given the success of the first three, I'm hoping we can offer to others going forward. I just have to figure out the details and how many I can take on."

"Yes, I know you'll have limited spots, so I have started to reach out to other restaurants to find anyone willing to do the same. When I mentioned you were doing it, I had two students picked up. One to A Dash and A Pinch, and one to Polly's Pizzeria. I have Mills Steakhouse interested and I have a meeting with Chef Nathan at Beaks and Brews in a few days."

"That is wonderful. I'm so glad to hear others are interested in doing it. All together, we can raise up wonderful new chefs." I smiled.

"All because of you."

Aunt Rita came into the living room with a tray with three mugs of hot tea and a batch of fresh oatmeal cookies. She had baked them earlier today, making the house smell wonderful.

We spent the next hour chatting about this or that, but nothing serious. I began to yawn, and my head started to spin a bit.

"Well, I will let you rest, but I'm so glad you are on the mend." He stood, giving my hand a squeeze.

"Thank you so much for coming. It truly was wonderful to see you."

"I'll walk you out," Rita said.

I laid my head back as I listened to them say goodbyes. I was asleep before she even had the door closed behind him. It was a few hours before I woke.

The house was quiet, and there was a note for me on the coffee table from Aunt Rita. She had left, but checking the time, my roommates should be home soon.

I went to clean myself up and use the bathroom before they arrived home. Unfortunately, I wasn't able to cook for us, so I think they planned to pick something up on the way home.

Back on the couch, I flipped through channels until I found something without a lot of flashing or action. It was an animal documentary.

The door opened and in came my roommates.

"We brought dinner!"

"Yay! My heroes."

"Beaks and Brew chicken with coleslaw and baked beans," Vee said. "Chef Nathan sends his thoughts to you. He threw in a dessert for free."

"Oh, yummy. That's so sweet of him. I'll have to send him a text later."

It was good to have friends. I was feeling the love.

"Are you up for sitting at the table, or do you want me to fix you a plate?"

"I would love to sit up."

"So, how was your visit with Mr. Jones?"

"It was nice. He told me a few other restaurants are open to having students come work with them."

"You're a trendsetter."

"You started a fad."

"I just want to help the students."

"You have a big heart."

Dinner was great, but afterwards, I was ready for bed. Vee came upstairs with me. She climbed into the bed with me so we could talk before I fell asleep.

"I am so glad you are okay," she said.

"Me too. That was so scary."

"It was so scary. When I first saw you, I was so worried."

"Well, I'm tough and not going to let these people win."

"I know you won't."

We laid there quietly. I woke hours later, alone in my room. I could hear Sawyer downstairs playing his game. Vee must be in her bed now. I can't believe I fell asleep talking.

Thankful for my friends and family, and so thankful to still be alive. Today had been a nice, boring, rest day. Just what I needed. I fell back asleep with a smile on my face.

Chapter Twenty-Three

Day one million and fifty of being home, stuck on the couch or bed. In reality, it was only seven days, but it just felt like more. Aunt Rita was still coming to make sure I was resting, and while I loved her, I was ready for her to go home, or get a hobby.

My headache wasn't getting better, though my body was healing nicely. It looked like my burns weren't going to leave much scarring, but still too early to tell for sure. But the doctor wanted me to continue resting each day and limit my screen time.

Today, I woke early to make breakfast for Sawyer and Vee before they left, and before Aunt Rita came to stop me, but I couldn't take it any longer. I needed to cook something.

I had nearly everything ready when my phone rang. The display showed Duncan Jones.

"Hello, Mr. Jones."

"Hi, Jessie. I hope I didn't wake you."

"No, not at all. I am making breakfast."

"Well, I wanted to … gosh, this isn't easy to say, but someone broke into the school overnight. They wrote a threat on the walls all over the classroom."

"What? Why? What does it say?"

"Stop helping Jessica or else you'll be next." His voice caught. "Jess, what is going on?"

I took a deep breath, not knowing how much to tell him, but knowing I couldn't hide this from him. He needed to know, especially now.

"I have been investigating the murder of a friend. He had found evidence that someone was embezzling money from the high school, mostly from the culinary arts program."

"What?"

"Yeah, seriously. It points to someone on the city council, but not sure who yet."

"So, your car exploding, not a malfunction?"

How did he figure that out? No point holding it all back now.

"Yes, it's related."

"Oh, Jessie."

"I'm so sorry that they came to you. I didn't think I had pointed any fingers your way. It should have all been at me."

"Maybe because I came by there the other day? Maybe because the money is being stolen from here?"

"Maybe so. What do you need me to do?" I asked.

"Nothing. I have already called the police, but while I was waiting, I thought I would call you since they named you."

"Well, okay."

"I'll let you know what they say."

"Again, I'm so sorry."

I choked back tears after we had hung up. This was not what I wanted. Come for me if they must, but my friends were another story. Mr. Jones was the sweetest, most caring person I knew. He didn't deserve to be harassed.

"Hey, good morning," Vee said, coming into the kitchen. "Are you okay?"

"You always know."

"Yeah, well." She shrugged.

"Mr. Jones just called. Someone broke into the school and painted a threat on the wall. It said to stop helping me."

"Oh, Jess." She gasped. "I hope we can solve this soon. I can't take more of these types of calls."

"Me neither."

Sawyer came downstairs then, all smiles and bed head.

"Good morning, ladies. Oh, friend, you made us breakfast!" He grabbed a plate, completely unaware that I was upset. That was one big difference between the two.

I chuckled to myself as I got a plate of food and joined him at the table. Vee got coffee first and then joined us with a plate.

My phone rang then. It was Detective Upton.

"Hi, Detective. I guess you're calling about the school." I saw Sawyer's head pop up and he mouthed to Vee, asking what happened. She gave him a minute sign as she turned her attention to listen.

"Yes, I wanted to come by later to interview you. Just see if you have any ideas."

"I'll be here all day. Doctor's orders."

"Yes, okay. By the way, how are you feeling?"

"Not awful, but not great."

"Well, I will keep my visit short. I'm just heading over to the school. Once I'm on my way to you, I'll text."

"Okay, sounds good."

I hung up and then looked at my friends. I really wished they could stay home with me today, but I knew they had to get to work.

"What happened?" Sawyer asked.

"Someone broke into the school. Mr. Jones called me earlier."

"What? Seriously?"

"Yeah, and Detective Upton is coming over later to talk with me."

"Does he think you are involved?"

"No, they painted a threat to Mr. Jones, pointing to me. Stop helping Jessica or you'll be next, or something like that."

He looked at me for a long second. "I'm going to take a day off."

He hopped up from the table before I could respond. I heard him in the other room on the phone. He came back a moment later.

"Alrighty, I'm yours for the day."

"What do you think is going to happen here?" I laughed.

"I don't know, but between you getting shot at, car exploding, and now this, I am just not taking chances with you today."

"Well, I'll be happy to have the extra company and a buffer between Aunt Rita."

"So, I'm the only one going to work today?" Vee pouted. "I would call in, too, but that would leave Rikki by herself on the desk. She is not as patient as I am."

We finished our breakfast and said goodbye to Vee. I settled into the couch for the day while Sawyer went to the office to stare at the board. He would yell out things to me occasionally.

"Should I take Riley down? You know since y'all talked."

"You can."

But I was keeping her on my list. Just because I could get past some of our issues didn't mean I wasn't still keeping one eye on her. It was too coincidental that she was there each time something happened. I wasn't saying she was the one who did anything, but she could have been sent as a distraction while the deeds were done.

"Do we have any theories on Chief Stone and Davis Campbell's meeting? We didn't write anything down for that."

"I don't know. It could have just been city council related and not something nefarious at all."

"That's true," he said. "I wish there was some clue in their pictures."

I could almost hear his gears turning from the other room. He wanted to solve this for my safety. It was a lot more dangerous than I had realized it would be. Who even knew I was asking questions? How could I have tipped anyone off? I needed to know, so I never repeated that mistake. Of course, I really hope this was the absolute last time that I investigated a murder.

He came back to the living room. "I'm not going to solve it that way. Do we still have the USB drives?"

"Yes, in the junk drawer. I put them in an envelope."

"Alrighty."

"I'm going to rest."

I laid my head back while he typed and clicked away on the computer. The sound was hypnotic. I dozed off quickly.

An hour later, I woke up to my Aunt Rita's voice.

"Sorry, sweetie, I didn't mean to wake you."

"Oh, it's okay. If I sleep too much, I'll be up all night."

"Do you need anything?"

"No, I think I'm okay."

"I'll make you some tea." She went to the kitchen. "Sawyer, do you want some tea?"

"No, Ms. Rita. I'm not a fan of hot tea," he said.

"I'll make you some hot chocolate."

He caught my eye, and we chuckled softly together. My aunt was a caring person, and she wasn't going to take no as an answer. She would always find another solution.

"By the way, Aunt Rita, Detective Upton will be stopping by at some point later."

"Oh, did they figure out who did this to you?"

"No, or not that I know of. He is coming by because someone broke into the culinary school, and he just wants to ask me some questions."

"Oh, my gosh. Who is doing all of this stuff? This town is going to heck in a handbag."

My phone rang. It was Noah, not the detective.

"Hey, Noah, what's up?"

"I just heard about the school. Are you okay?"

"Yeah, I'm fine. I mean, worried, of course, but I'm safe. Sawyer stayed home from work and Aunt Rita is here."

"Okay, do you want me to come over after Cullen gets here? We can go through the clues again."

"Yeah, that might be helpful. Sawyer is going back through the USB drives and files today, just to see if we missed a clue."

"Great. I'll call you later."

We hung up, and I relayed the message to Sawyer.

"Perfect. I haven't found anything new yet, but there are a lot of files here. I can't believe how long this has been going on. Did Colt say anything else in his emails and notes?"

"They were vague. He just said he was close to figuring out who and these files should get us there."

"Did I hear you say that Noah is coming by later?" Aunt Rita asked, setting my tea on the coffee table.

"Yes, so we can go through this case together. We must be close to an answer."

"Do you really think this is a good idea? You were almost killed. Is that worth it?"

"I think it will be okay. We aren't doing anything crazy. Just hanging out in our house." I tried to assure her.

Of course, there was the man who had come by with a gun that one night. It had given me pause at the naïve sense of safety I had at home. Maybe I shouldn't feel so flippant about being okay here.

"Well, you need to rest and not be too active."

"I know. I will be still most of the day."

"Okay, but I'm going to ensure you do," Aunt Rita said firmly. She grabbed her bag with her book in it, then plopped down on the far side of the couch.

Sawyer worked on the computer for another hour. Anytime he tried to get me involved, Aunt Rita would run him off. Instead of talking to me, he would run back and forth between the computer and the board. At some point, he moved into the office.

I dozed on and off until my phone rang just after lunch.

"Hi, Detective, are you on your way?"

"No, bad news. I'm stuck over here and then Chief Stone wants me back at the station. I wanted to see if I could come by tomorrow."

"Yeah, okay, that's fine."

His comment about Chief Stone had me a bit concerned. Did he know that Detective Upton had planned to come talk to me? Was that why he was called back to the mother ship?

"Well, I'll call you tomorrow to set up a time."

"Great." I hung up and stared at the phone for a moment. I really was tired of this dragging out, but my days were quite boring without visitors. Tomorrow I will have at least one.

"He isn't coming?" Aunt Rita asked.

"Nope, not today."

"Good. One less distraction. You need to rest."

"Yes, ma'am."

"Sassy, girl." She chuckled, tapping my foot with her book. "You know I'm right."

"Yes, you are."

An hour later, Noah called to cancel.

"Detective Upton wants to talk to me tomorrow. He asked if I could meet him at your place sometime in the afternoon."

"Really? Weird. He called me earlier to ask about coming tomorrow."

"Well, I hope he has answers about Colt."

"Me too. Well, see you tomorrow then."

Aunt Rita was thrilled to hear that nobody was coming.

"My job here is done. I'll bring your meds and a fresh glass of water before I leave."

I chuckled as she did the last chore before leaving for the evening. She brought over my pills.

"Rest up, sweetie. I love you." She kissed my head as she went out the door.

She was my guardian and protector. I was a lucky person.

Chapter Twenty-Four

"So, what do you think the detective wants from us?" Mr. Jones asked.

"No idea, but since he asked for all three of us to be here, it must be news about Colt, the attacks on me, and how it relates to the break in at the school," I said.

All of that was probably obvious, but I didn't know what else to say. I was nervous that he wouldn't have an answer.

Noah nodded but didn't say anything.

There was a knock on the door. The three of us exchanged a look. Aunt Rita had an appointment today then was volunteering with Granny Ines at the nursing home, which worked out perfectly to have the detective over. I didn't need her worrying and flitting about us while we tried to talk.

"I'll get it," Noah said, popping up. He pulled the door open. "Good morning, Detective. Come in."

"Thank you." Detective Upton looked across the room to where Mr. Jones and I were sitting. "Good morning. Thank you all for meeting with me."

"We hope you have good news."

"Um, no, unfortunately, not yet, but I just had questions about what you two have been up to and what Duncan can share with us about anyone who might have done this."

Noah looked at me with a look I could almost read. He was thinking about our clue board in the other room. I was thankful that the detective couldn't see into our office right now. He might not like that we did that.

"Okay, we'll let you know what we can," I said, fighting the urge to look over my shoulder towards the office.

"Well, I guess first, what have you two been up to? Who have you spoken to?"

"Um, okay, well." I was stalling. "You know that I spoke to Imogen Potter, but not about Colt. Then we spoke to April, who you know is Colt's sister."

"Not those people. Who have you been upsetting?"

"I don't know. If I knew that, I would have already told you."

The detective sighed heavily. "Okay, let me word this differently. Where have you been going?"

"Well, the apartment building, the city council meeting, and the school mostly. I have been to city hall twice now. Once to find out about when the council meeting was and the next to attend the meeting."

I left off going to the postal boxes to get the first USB drive and how I went to Colt's apartment a few times to snoop. Only the first and last time, I didn't get to search at all. I don't count the time we packed up his apartment because I had been invited that time.

"So, why were you there with Ms. Imogen Potter?"

I had already told him this, so I'd just make sure I told him the same story. I mean it was mostly true.

"I went to just confirm that he was really gone. I had no plan or anything. Just couldn't believe what happened." That was the truth, more or less. I had kind of hoped that I could sneak in and look around, but then didn't know what to do once I was there. "I was standing staring at his door, and she came from her apartment. She told me he had died and then we walked down together."

"Okay. And you'd never met her before then?"

"No, I'd never even been inside of Beck Apartments until that day."

"Okay. Then with city hall, who did you talk to and see there?"

"I saw Superintendent Van Rhodes the first time, then when I went back for the council meeting, I saw ... well, the city council members."

"Was Chief Stone there?"

"Yes, and we talked. I also talked to Van Rhodes again that night."

"Okay, okay." He scribbled everything I said down.

He then moved on to asking Noah questions. I half listened, but mostly I thought about what I had said. Could anything be mistaken or taken wrong? Had I given too much information?

I couldn't understand why he was asking us so many questions instead of being out there looking for clues and the people behind all of this. We were lawful members of society, and with a few exceptions of attempted snooping, I hadn't done anything wrong.

I started listening again as Noah was talking about the funeral.

"They did a slideshow of his life. It was beautiful, but no, I don't remember anything weird in the pictures. However, during the graveside service, there were two guys that I didn't recognize. They were wearing dark shades, standing away from most guests."

"Did you talk to them?"

"No, I was busy with the family. April and Emmie, Colt's mom, were upset, so I was comforting them."

"And you weren't with Jess at Beck Apartment when she met Imogen Potter."

"No."

Detective Upton looked at me but didn't say anything. He made a note, read back through them, and then looked over at Noah.

"Did you go with her either time to city hall?"

"No, I didn't, though I was going to attend the council meeting, but something came up last minute."

"What came up?"

"The Evans family needed me, mostly April, but we ended up at Ralph and Emmie's for dinner. Some of the rest of the family came over as well. It turned into almost a second memorial for Colt. We just sat around playing cards and reminiscing about good ole days."

"Sounds nice," Detective Upton said as he made notes.

"It was."

"Okay, well, it really sounds like she has been the main person looking into things." Detective Upton glared at me, his eyes lingering on the burns on my arms and face.

"I'm sorry. He was a nice guy, and I didn't want his killer to get away." I smiled sheepishly.

"But, according to you, you didn't even know him that well." He paused. "So, why is this so important to you?"

I thought I just answered that question, but I know he wanted the real reason. Looking at Noah, I wish I could have a sidebar conversation with him. It didn't seem like my place to talk about the email and the USB drives, the blurry pictures, or the financial records.

Plus, if this did point back to Chief Stone, I did not know who else at the police station was involved. Could Detective Upton be involved? My friend Rafferty? I didn't know.

"The honest truth is, I didn't want him to be forgotten. The killer is getting away with this and if it was the same people who have been going after me, they are still out there, trying to hurt people." Tears formed in my eyes. My pain was a reminder. Not to mention the loss of my car.

"Okay, then." He nodded. "Now, Duncan, have you been doing any digging into this?"

"I didn't even know there was anything going on. They came to talk to me about a partnership. I gave them recommendations on students, and they hired them as apprentices. Other than that, we haven't had much contact. Though I have eaten a few times at The Crock Pot and ran into her around town a few times a year."

"Who knew that you had met with them?"

"My students, the school secretary, and my wife, Beverly."

Duncan Jones's mention of Shirley Wolfe knowing had me thinking about the board again. I have seen her more in the last month than I had in the past twenty years. Could I be wrong about her?

I had no proof, and it didn't seem fair to just point a finger her way. She hadn't done anything, and she wasn't even at the city council meeting. She'd only seen me at the school then stopped by the house to drop off some pictures. Then there was the day at the grocery store, but lots of people go to the grocery store.

That was it. Nothing that made me think she was involved, so I kept my mouth shut on my thoughts. It would just muddy the already dark waters of this investigation.

"Um, okay." He wrote another note. "I guess that's all I need."

"Okay." Noah stood to walk him out. "Thank you for coming."

Mr. Jones and I sat quietly as we watched the detective leave, and Noah shut the door behind him. He let out a sigh as he turned back to us.

"Why do I feel you are the suspect in this?" he said, sitting back down with us. He looked at me.

"Okay. Glad I'm not the only one who thought that."

"I didn't realize all of this was going on. I mean, you explained some of it yesterday, but wow. Are you in danger?" Mr. Jones asked.

"I don't think so." But I honestly didn't know. I'd been shot at and my car blown up, so the reality was I probably was.

"Well, I am going to get home. Beverly will be nervous with all this going on." He leaned over to hug me, then Noah walked him out.

Now it was just the two of us. He sank down into the chair.

"That didn't go well," he said. "I had really hoped he would have answers for us, but with Chief Stone potentially involved, it's no surprise."

"Yeah, I thought about that, too. I also wondered what he would have thought if we showed him our board."

"I know. It was on the tip of my tongue to show it to him, but then I thought about Chief Stone."

"That was exactly my thought."

"Great minds," he said. We chuckled.

I studied him for a minute, trying to decide if I should let him in on the rest of my thoughts.

"Do you think it could be the school secretary, Shirley Wolfe?"

"Really? Why do you think that?"

"When Mr. Jones was talking about who knew we had talked to him, he mentioned her, and it just was a thought."

"Honestly, anything is possible. Should we go look at the clue board?"

"Yeah, let's. Maybe we can add some notes."

We walked into the other room, staring at the board. I grabbed a sticky note adding "knew we were at the school" then stuck it under Shirley's name. Under Chief Stone, Van Rhodes, and Davis Campbell I stuck a note saying "knew I was at the city council meeting."

"Did I miss anything?"

He looked over his shoulder. "Would Sawyer be upset if we added a note that Riley was at the restaurant each time something happened to your car?"

I half laughed. "Yeah, probably but you keep reading my mind. That just seems too much of a coincidence, right?"

"It really does. She was pretty rude that one night, too."

"Yeah, but rude doesn't necessarily mean guilty."

"True, true." He rubbed his chin. "I feel like it's right there."

"Yes, what are we missing?"

We stood there for several more minutes before he turned to look at me.

"How are you feeling? Your head?"

"It's okay. I'll probably nap later." I didn't tell him how bad it was pounding right now, and I was having some dizziness.

"Alright, do you need anything before I hit the road?" he asked.

"Um, I think I'm good. Thank you."

With that, he left, and I was alone for the first time in nearly a week. My roommates were at work. Aunt Rita wasn't here, so I decided to nap on the couch and forget about the board, the murder, and how crazy my life was.

Chapter Twenty-Five

I'd gone to my doctor yesterday for a follow-up and he'd extended my recovery time. He wasn't happy with how I was healing, or should I say lack of healing.

"You're burns and scrapes look good. They are healing well. How is your head?"

I hesitated for a moment, thinking perhaps I should lie. I knew I hadn't been as quiet, calm, and limiting screen time as I should. Lying would only hurt me in the long run.

"I'm still getting headaches, having some difficulty with concentrating, and still getting some dizziness."

"Are you resting?"

"I'm trying."

"Umph." He looked at me. "Well, I need you to do better."

He sentenced me to another week at home as punishment for not resting more. I was going a bit stir crazy being at home. Vee gave me a stern lecture again this morning on her way out the door.

"Stay on the couch except to go to the restroom. Period."

"But what if I need water?"

She sighed heavily as she rolled her eyes at me. "You know what I mean. No reorganizing the kitchen. No laundry. No outside visitors, except your Aunt Rita. I will do anything you want when I get home. Stay. Watch TV, but nothing too wild. Rest up."

"Yes, mom!" I stuck out my tongue.

She laughed. "You're a sassy child."

Sawyer just stood back, laughing at us both. They waved and were gone for the day. I looked around. It was quiet. I was used to the buzz, clinks, and clanks of the kitchen. Another week without it would be difficult, but I could do it. I had no choice.

Exhaling, I fell back onto the couch. Grabbing the remote, I flipped to the food channel. Maybe I couldn't cook, but I could watch other people cooking.

I watched television for a bit but got bored quickly with it. I grabbed my laptop, thinking that I could go through Colt's files again, even though Sawyer had already done it. With all the attention and attacks, plus the extra time on my hands, I was set on getting this resolved now.

An hour later, my head was starting to hurt, but I was determined. I popped a few painkillers, and continued the search, moving from the couch to the kitchen island to give me a different point of view.

Another hour of clicking, before I slammed the laptop closed, then massaged my temples. That's when I got a weird text message from Mr. Jones saying, "Help!" but I had no idea what that meant. Where was he?

Me: **Where are you?**

No reply, and the message went unread. I paced around, trying to decide what to do. Should I call the police? But I didn't know where to send them or if he really needed help. Was it just helping the students? Help with a decision?

I stopped pacing as a wave of lightheadedness came over me. Checking the time, I couldn't wait too long to decide. Even though it was a Friday, it was a school holiday, but knowing Mr. Jones, he was likely at the school prepping lessons and taking inventory.

Exhaling heavily, I grabbed Vee's car keys since they had taken Sawyer's to work. I would start at the school and then go from there. If I couldn't find him on my own, I would call the police then.

I hadn't driven much in the past two weeks, so the first few miles felt a little strange, but soon I felt more comfortable. I got close to the school when my nerves started to kick in. As I pulled into the parking lot, I recognized his car right away, but there were a few others that I didn't.

Parking near his car, I sat there for a moment trying to decide what to do. If he was in trouble, I couldn't wait for the police to arrive. However, I also couldn't go charging in because what could I really do?

"Come on, Jess, make a decision," I said to myself.

Alright, I could call it in to 9-1-1, but then while they are on the way, I would go inside. With my choice made, I placed the call.

"And what kind of danger is he in?"

"I'm not sure. He sent me a text that said help. He hasn't read my reply yet, and his car is in the parking lot at the school."

"Do you see anyone there?"

"No, but there are a couple of other cars in the parking lot."

"Okay, I have dispatched an officer to your location. Please stay in your car and they will meet you there," she instructed.

Her tone gave me little confidence that she'd dispatched anyone. She sounded like she didn't believe me. She spoke as if she was pacifying the boy who cried wolf.

"Okay."

But I had no intention of staying in my car. I just didn't tell her that part, though it might cause her to dispatch someone sooner.

One more minute to gather my courage, and hope that the police came soon. I climbed out of the car, putting my phone on silent, then headed in. Maybe Shirley was at the desk and could help me.

I got to the front doors, only to find them locked. I peered in but didn't see anyone. I looked in the office windows, but it was dark inside. I made my way around to the first set of side doors. These lead into the cosmetology room, but they were locked. Next, I went to the computer labs, locked. After those was the mechanic shop. Bingo! These were open.

I crept in, trying to see in the dark, unfamiliar room. I'd never spent time in the shop, so I had no idea the layout. My head spun as I tried to force all my senses into overtime. My ears were trying to pick up each sound. My eyes darted to take in each shadow. My nose tried to smell anything unusual. I reached my hands forward, feeling my way through the room.

Reaching the door that would lead me into the hallway. I hesitated a second before opening it, as I listened for any noise. Not hearing anything, I slowly opened the door, peeking out. The culinary classroom and Mr. Jones's office were just a few doors down. The hallway was silent and dimly lit.

I stepped out, creeping against the wall, trying to stay low in case anyone was watching me. As I got close to the culinary arts room, I could hear a loud male voice.

He sounded angry.

"Tell me what she knows!"

That was followed by a muffled voice. I couldn't hear them. *Bleep! I think that is Mr. Jones.*

I crept closer, trying to will my ears to hear better. The police should be here by now, but would they know how to get inside? I backed up and went into the mechanic room again so I could text Detective Upton, then ensured my phone was still on silent.

I looked around the room again, grabbing a large wrench from a nearby workstation, then made my way back to the culinary room again. I stood outside the door.

"He obviously knows nothing. Just kill him and let's go after her again," a female voice said. Her voice was familiar, but I couldn't place it.

"You said she looks up to him and he was a mentor. He was over there twice this week, along with that manager of hers."

"Well, I just want to kill him and finally be done with him," the female voice said.

Wait? I do know that voice. That's Shirley Wolfe, the school secretary. Now it all made sense. She was the key to all of this. She had a relationship with the school and with the superintendent. That's why she didn't need to be at the city council meeting because he was there.

Oh, bleep, that is the other voice. Superintendent Van Rhodes.

He had access to the accounts and budget, so together they could siphon money from the school, and nobody would notice. But how did Chief Stone and Davis Campbell factor in? Is that why the police weren't here yet?

I pulled my phone from my pocket to check if there were any messages from Detective Upton. Pulling it out, I saw there were a few missed calls and several texts. Unfortunately, I fumbled as I tried to unlock my phone. I watched helplessly as it went flying out of my hands, in slow motion, and across the hallway. It landed with a clank that echoed through the empty school.

A curse sounded from inside the culinary room, and then loud footsteps came my way. I had nowhere to go, but I pushed back as far and as fast as I could back down the hallway, trying to make it to the mechanic room.

"Stop. Right. There." Superintendent Rhodes growled.

I looked over to see him aiming a gun at me. Instinctively, my hands went up. A wicked grin slowly spread across his face.

"I guess I just needed to be patient and you would come to me." He motioned the gun for me to get up. "Why don't you join us in here?"

He pushed me forward as Shirley Wolfe stood in the doorway, arms folded over her chest.

"Well, look what the cat dragged in." She laughed.

In the classroom, I saw they had Duncan Jones tied up and blindfolded. He had a bloody lip and looked lethargic as his head hung limp.

"What did you do to him?"

"We did what we had to, but it doesn't matter. You're here. That's what we really wanted. You," Van Rhodes said.

"I don't understand what you want with me. I'm nobody."

Shirley laughed a wicked, high-pitched laugh. It sent chills to my soul.

"You have all the files from that boy," he snarled. "We almost had it, but that oaf of a lackey we had fell down on the job."

"That's why we had him taken out." She laughed again.

"I don't have anything. I don't even know what you're talking about," I said firmly.

They exchanged a look, then looked at me, sizing me up as if trying to decide if they believed me or not. Obviously, it was a lie, but I was hoping they bought it. I kept my face as neutral as possible, hoping to fool them with my bluff.

"She's lying!" Shirley snapped. She lunged at me, but thankfully I wasn't tied up like Mr. Jones. I dodged, causing her to tumble forward.

Van Rhodes fired a shot but thankfully missed as I dove behind a cook station. I crawled along the floor, trying to put as much distance between me and him as I could. I was not going out this way.

My head was ringing from my concussion, but I was determined to get out of this alive.

"Come on, Ms. Chef, come out, come out," Van taunted. I could hear his footsteps stalking me.

"Where is she?" Shirley shrieked. "Over there!"

A shot fired above me again. I jumped and kept crawling from station to station until I circled back around to Mr. Jones. I checked on him. Thankfully, he was breathing, but he was in bad shape. They had really knocked him around.

Looking over my shoulder, Van and I made eye contact.

Bleep!

I grabbed Mr. Jones as best I could. He could barely keep his feet under him, but we ran from the room. We stumbled out into the hallway and right into a wall of police officers. I saw Rafferty, Roberts, Lopez, Upton, and Chief Stone.

Rafferty grabbed us, moving us further down the hallway, just as Superintendent Van Rhodes and Mrs. Shirley Wolfe came out of the room with guns in hand. They saw the officers, letting out a line of curses, and their hands went up.

The officers jumped into action.

I sighed with relief as I saw them taken into custody. This was finally going to be over, and Colt's killers would be brought to justice.

Chief Stone stepped over to me. "You are one lucky girl, you know that?"

"I suppose."

"Well, thank you for calling dispatch. If not for your tip, they would have continued to get away with their scheme."

"You knew about it?"

"Most of it, but not all. We have been trying to get these two for a while. Davis Campbell and I had been meeting about it but couldn't quite nail down the who." The chief stuck his hand forward as if to shake my hand. "You did it. Thank you."

My mouth fell open. Chief Stone was thanking me. Me. I slowly took his hand, shaking it as I processed what he said.

"Wait? We have … I saw pictures with you and Davis Campbell together. It was for this? Them?"

"Yes, well, not as far as you got. We knew only that someone was skimming off the school's budget. We couldn't quite find the who and that's why we had Colt Evans helping us. Shame they got to him. I will forever feel guilt for that one."

"Oh, wow." Colt was working for them. "Well, glad we could get them stopped. But why you and not one of your detectives or officers? I thought chiefs were more of the behind the desk, managing things type. Not investigating or on the street job."

"Normally, yes, that's true, but this case required someone that could be at some high-level meetings. A bit of a political role, if you will." He nodded slightly, as if I was supposed to understand. I guess I did. He was part of the city council and could be in all of those meetings with the superintendent and school board.

"It makes sense."

Detective Upton came over, nodding at Chief Stone. "How are you feeling, Jess? Do we need the EMTs to check you as well?"

My head was pounding, and my stomach was churning. They were already attending to Mr. Jones. It looked like he was going to be okay. He was now talking, though still a little out of it.

"Yeah, I better get checked out."

Detective Upton signaled to one of the EMTs to check me. They decided that we should both be transported to the hospital for further treatment.

All I knew was Colt's murder was solved and he had not been doing anything shady after all. I know that Noah was worried about what Colt had been working on. His dad, Ralph had hinted that he thought Colt was doing bad things, so this was going to be good news to all of them.

Chapter Twenty-Six

It had been a week since the scandal broke. I had, finally, been released to go back to work. It felt so good to use those cooking muscles again.

"Shrimp and grits, and a chicken fried steak," Hannah yelled out.

I got to work on the dishes, sautéing the onions and peppers, then added in the garlic and shrimp. Got the chicken fried steak into the fryer, then plated the mashed potatoes and green beans. Once it was all ready, I plated it and put it up for a runner.

"Order," I yelled out.

I sighed with satisfaction. I sure missed this. Another order came in so I got back to work on cooking.

An hour later, Jordan came to my station.

"Chef, Nadine is here for your interview."

Nadine wrote a local foodie blog called Dining with Nadine. She wanted to come do an updated article about me and our biscuits.

"Thanks, Jordan. Let her know I'll be right there," I said. "Oh, wait? Did she order something?"

"Just a drink, but I brought her some biscuits and your blackberry jam. She was happy with that."

"Oh, good!" I wanted word to get out about our biscuits. Parker had done an amazing job of creating them, and so far, they'd been a hit.

I washed up, then headed to the dining room, stopping first for a peach lemonade.

"Thanks, Ripley." I tipped the drink in his direction.

Scanning the dining room, I saw Nadine sitting at a booth close to the front of the restaurant. I made my way to her, being stopped by customers along the way.

"Hi, Chef, so glad to have you back."

"You look good. Glad you're feeling better."

"We really missed you around here."

They were all so sweet to say that. I thanked them as I walked past. It felt so good to be loved here in the community, and that they found value in me and noticed my absence.

"Hi, Nadine. It's good to see you again," I said, taking a seat across from her.

"You, too. I'm so glad you're okay."

"So, how did you enjoy the biscuits and jam?"

"These are the best biscuits. Savory but work with the sweet jam. Crispy, yet soft."

"I'm glad you enjoy them. They are the creation of Chef Parker Rowe."

"Oh, nice." She licked her fingers and then made a note. "Okay, okay, so tell me, how is Duncan Jones?"

"He is okay. He had a black eye, a broken nose, and a busted lip, but he is thankful to be safe."

"We're all thankful. He is a special person to our town." She looked at me. "And we're really glad you are okay as well."

"Thank you. Yes, all recovered."

"I can't believe you figured out who was behind all of this. How did you figure it out?"

"I just got lucky, really."

I'd been told by the chief and Detective Upton not to say too much about how this all came together. They needed to finish building the case against Van Rhodes and Shirley Wolfe.

"You'll get a lot of questions. Be as vague as possible," Chief Stone coached me. "We'll have our department give a more detailed report later."

I smiled thinking about the change in our relationship. Chief Stone was still not my favorite person, but I had a new respect for him.

"Well, you've solved two cases now. We should start calling you the crime fighting chef!"

"Ha, wouldn't that be funny, but no, I was just at the right places at the right times."

We continued to chat back and forth. It was nice to talk shop and sit in my restaurant, watching my customers come and go, watching my staff move around. I simply smiled, taking it all in.

"I think I have enough to add an article about you and the restaurant on my blog. I think you'll be happy with it."

"I'm sure I will. Thank you."

I walked her out and then went to finish my shift.

The apprentices arrived around two. I was so happy to see them.

"Thank you for saving Mr. Jones."

"We really appreciate you."

"We are so happy you're back."

"Thanks. I'm glad to be back and so glad that I found Mr. Jones, too."

They had now been here long enough that I didn't need to get them started. They jumped right in as if they were seasoned pros. I watched for a moment. They'd come a long way in the last few weeks while I was out.

"Hey, Chef," Parker said, coming in. "Is that your new car out there?"

"Yeah. I got red instead of blue."

"It's nice."

I had never bought a new car before, I'd found the process both exciting and overwhelming. Granny Ines had gone with me.

"I know a guy," she had said. "His grandmother is in my Bible study group."

He gave me a great deal. It was good to have connections.

"Thanks. Well, everyone is doing their thing. Nothing special to report from the day. Thank goodness."

"Good. We like boring."

"Yes, we do."

I headed to the office, finding that Noah was still here.

"Oh, I thought you'd left."

"We just finished up, so I was just heading out," Noah said.

"I'll walk out with you." I grabbed my purse and waved goodbye to Cullen.

Out in the parking lot, I had a flashback of the last time I walked out this door. The flash of light, the searing pain, and the ball of fire that was my car were all burned into my brain.

"Are you thinking about it?"

"Yeah."

"It was scary. I've watched the footage a few times."

"Really?"

"Yes, the police wanted it."

"Ah, makes sense." I looked at him. "How are the Evans?"

"They are so glad that this is solved, especially knowing Colt was doing something good, and not nefarious. They appreciate everything you did."

"Everything we did."

"I didn't do nearly as much as you did. Thank you for giving us all closure."

We hugged then said our goodbyes. I stood there only a moment before hopping in my new car, then heading home.

For the millionth time today, I thought how wonderful it was to be back in my normal routine, and I really hoped this was the last time I had to solve a murder.

THE END

Before you go: If you loved Biscuits and Bodies, be sure to visit my website to sign up for my newsletter (if you haven't already) and to stay up to date on new releases and other bookish things. When signing up, you will receive **Chef Jessica's Alphabet Soup Recipe** as a free gift. I have "had" it, it is yummy. (Okay, so obviously, it is my recipe, but still, I recommend it!) Continue to the next section for this book's recipe!

www.ejwheltonwrites.com

Recipe:

This is now my go-to biscuit recipe. My hubby loves them!

Drop biscuits:

- 2 cups all-purpose flour
- 1 tablespoon baking powder
- 1 ¼ teaspoon kosher salt
- ½ teaspoon black pepper (I use coarse)
- ½ cup (1 stick) cold unsalted butter, cut into small pieces (I usually freeze it for about 20-30 minutes before)
- 1 cup milk (or buttermilk)
- ½ grated cheddar cheese (freshly grated, not pre-grated)

Instructions:

1. Preheat the oven to 450 F (232 C).
2. In a large bowl, whisk together flour, baking powder, black pepper and salt together.
3. Add grated cheese. Fold in to coat it with the flour mixture.
4. Add the pieces of cold butter and cut into the dry ingredients with a pastry cutter or fork until the consistency of coarse meal.
5. Add milk a little at a time, stirring until it is combined (You may not need the full cup). If the batter is very dry, add a little more milk until the consistency of a very thick batter. If too sticky, sprinkle with a bit of flour but only enough so it is not too sticky. Do not over-mix. It will be quite thick, almost like you could roll it out.
6. Drop large mounds (about 1/4 cup each. You can use a 2 oz scoop but I use my hands, making them golf ball sized) onto a baking sheet.
7. Bake at 450 F (232 C) for 16-18 minutes until golden brown
8. Brush with melted butter if desired.

They will be crispy on the outside but soft on the inside. Enjoy with your favorite jelly, jam, or preserve (whatever you like, but I like strawberry)!!
If you make it email me at ejwheltonwrites@gmail.com and let me know what you think.

Author note:

Another fun one to write! What is crazy to me is just as Jess was learning about Colt, so was I. I really liked him as a person (character) and was sad that he had to die.

I want to thank my parents, my husband, my children, and my dear, dear friends for all their support once again with this one.

And a special shout out to Mariah Sinclair for the gorgeous cover! She took my vision and brought it to life.

Now on to Cornbread and Coffins! Jess is going to take a catering job, something she doesn't do. Once again, she's thrust into role of sleuth when an unexpected body is found.

Thank you for reading and for your amazing support.

www.ejwheltonwrites.com

www.ingramcontent.com/pod-product-compliance
Lightning Source LLC
Chambersburg PA
CBHW031752200726
48289CB00013B/804